D0540453

INFOGRAPHIC

|||||||||||||||||||||||||||||||||||||||||||||| **GUIDE TO** ||||||||||||||||||||||||||||||||||||||||||||||

LITERATURE

An Hachette UK Company
www.hachette.co.uk

First published in Great Britain in 2014 by Cassell Illustrated
a division of Octopus Publishing Group Ltd

Endeavour House
189 Shaftesbury Avenue
London
WC2H 8JY

www.octopusbooks.co.uk
www.octopusbooksusa.com

Copyright © Essential Works Ltd 2014

Distributed in the US by
Hachette Book Group USA
237 Park Avenue
New York NY 10017 USA

Distributed in Canada by
Canadian Manda Group
664 Annette Street
Toronto, Ontario, Canada M6S 2C8

All rights reserved. No part of this work may be reproduced or utilized in any
form or by any means, electronic or mechanical, including photocopying,
recording or by any information storage and retrieval system, without the prior
written permission of the publisher.

Essential Works Ltd asserts the moral right to
be identified as the author of this work.

ISBN 978-1-844037-87-2

A CIP catalogue record for this book is available from the British Library

Printed and bound in China

1 3 5 7 9 10 8 6 4 2

LONDON BOROUGH OF HACKNEY LIBRARIES	
HK12002391	
Bertrams	06/02/2015
802	£12.99
	06/10/2014

INFOGRAPHIC

||||||||||||||||||||||||||||||||| GUIDE TO |||||||||||||||||||||||||||||||||

LITERATURE

Joanna Eliot

CONTENTS

CRIMINA...

When Agatha Christie...
public in 1930, she beg...
female detectives. Per...
been Patricia Cornwel...
counts for the 12 Miss...
idea of how the worl...

...ISS MARPLE MISS M...

AGATHA CHRIST...
b.1890, Devon...
d.1976, Oxfords...
England

LITERARY **MISERY** INDEX

In 2013, researchers at University College London and Bristol University checked the occurrence of words that denoted misery in five million English-language works published between 1900 and 2000. They then checked their findings against the economically-based US Misery Index which charts unemployment and inflation. It seems that books get more miserable a decade after the world has undergone a depression.

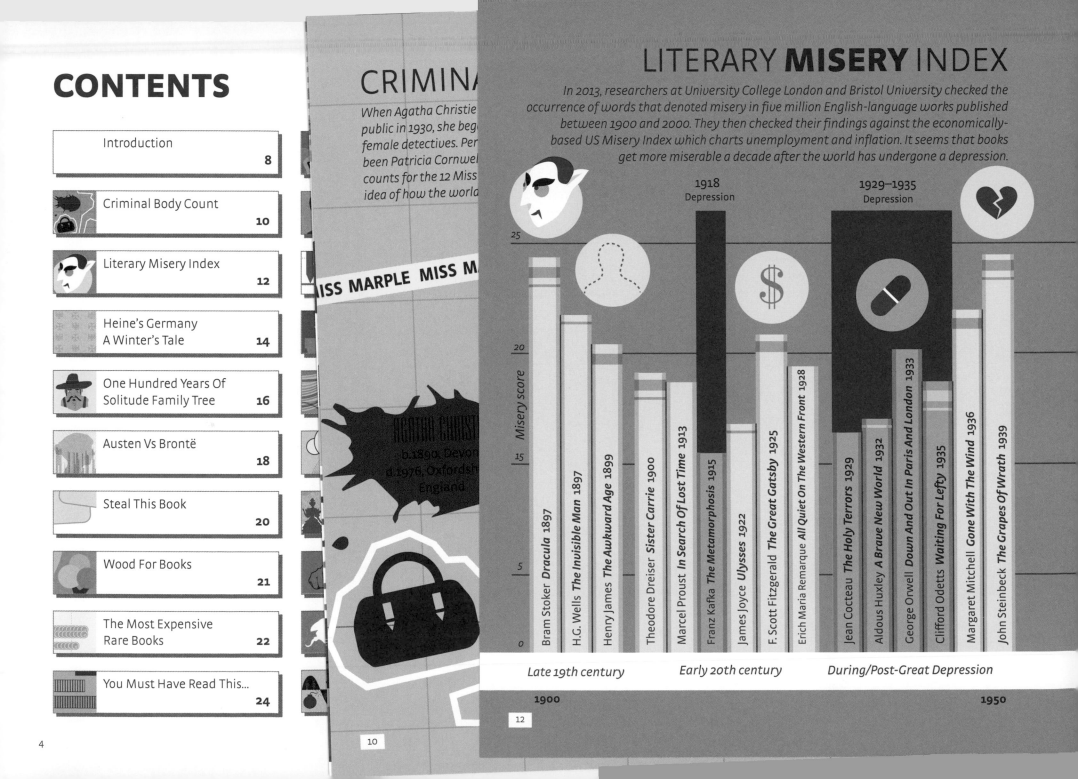

1918
Depression

1929–1935
Depression

Misery score

25

20

15

5

0

- Bram Stoker *Dracula* 1897
- H.G. Wells *The Invisible Man* 1897
- Henry James *The Awkward Age* 1899
- Theodore Dreiser *Sister Carrie* 1900
- Marcel Proust *In Search Of Lost Time* 1913
- Franz Kafka *The Metamorphosis* 1915
- James Joyce *Ulysses* 1922
- F. Scott Fitzgerald *The Great Gatsby* 1925
- Erich Maria Remarque *All Quiet On The Western Front* 1928
- Jean Cocteau *The Holy Terrors* 1929
- Aldous Huxley *A Brave New World* 1932
- George Orwell *Down And Out In Paris And London* 1933
- Clifford Odetts *Waiting For Lefty* 1935
- Margaret Mitchell *Gone With The Wind* 1936
- John Steinbeck *The Grapes Of Wrath* 1939

Late 19th century   *Early 20th century*   *During/Post-Great Depression*

1900   1950

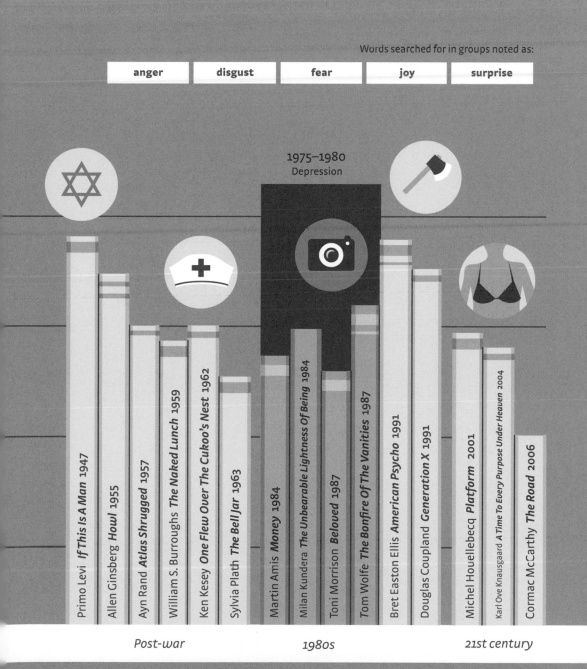

Words searched for in groups noted as:

anger | **disgust** | **fear** | **joy** | **surprise**

1975–1980
Depression

Primo Levi *If This Is A Man* 1947

Allen Ginsberg *Howl* 1955

Ayn Rand *Atlas Shrugged* 1957

William S. Burroughs *The Naked Lunch* 1959

Ken Kesey *One Flew Over The Cukoo's Nest* 1962

Sylvia Plath *The Bell Jar* 1963

Martin Amis *Money* 1984

Milan Kundera *The Unbearable Lightness Of Being* 1984

Toni Morrison *Beloved* 1987

Tom Wolfe *The Bonfire Of The Vanities* 1987

Bret Easton Ellis *American Psycho* 1991

Douglas Coupland *Generation X* 1991

Michel Houellebecq *Platform* 2001

Karl Ove Knausgård *A Time To Every Purpose Under Heaven* 2004

Cormac McCarthy *The Road* 2006

Post-war | *1980s* | *21st century*

1950 | 2000

Bentley RA, Acerbi A, Ormerod P, Lampos V (2014) Books Average Previous Decade of Economic Misery.
PLoS ONE 9(1): e83147. doi:10.1371/journal.pone.0083147

13

HEINE'S GERMANY:
A WINTER'S TALE

The work of German-Jewish poet Heinrich Heine was banned in his homeland in 1835. In 1844, inspired by composer Schubert's Die Winterreise, *Heine published* Deutschland: Ein Wintermärchen, *an imaginary journey through his homeland in poetic form. Here's where he went and the symbolic items of each section.*

MINDEN **14**

TEUTOBURG FOREST **10**

BUCKEBURG **15**

WESTPHALIA **9**

MULHEIM **8**

PADERBORN **11**

7 HAGEN

COLOGNE **5** **6**

AACHEN **2**

3

THE RHINELAND **4**

1
PARIS

Section I, II **1**

Section III **2**

Section IV **3**

Section V **4**

Section VI **5**

Section VII **6**

Section X **9**

Section XI, XII **10**

Section XIII **11**

Section IV, V **12**

Section VI, XVII **13**

Section XVIII **14**

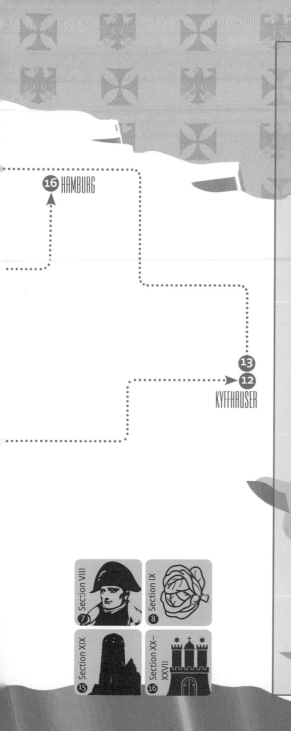

16 HAMBURG

13
12
KYFFHÄUSER

wikipedia.org

KEY TO SYMBOLS

1 START: (Section I, II) Paris; Heine sets out on an imaginary journey to real places.

2 (Section III) Aachen; lands in Germany carrying shirts, trousers, handkerchiefs in a suitcase and books in his head.

3 (Section IV) Travels the road from Aachen to Cologne, and at Cologne Cathedral applauds the unfinished building as showing Germany's progressive society.

4 (Section V) In the Rhineland, Heine sees old Father Rhine as sad and disappointed with Germans concerned about their identity.

5 (Section VI) Cologne; Heine shows 'Liktor' a demon who is always with him and carries a hatchet under his cloak.

6 (Section VII) At Cologne Cathedral Heine smashes the 'skeletons of superstition'.

7 (Section VIII) Hagen; Heine recalls seeing Napoleon Bonaparte's funeral.

8 (Section IX) Mulheim; Heine recalls the taste of great sauerkraut.

9 (Section X) Heine sends his regards to Westphalia.

10 (Section XI, XII) Heine travels through Teutoburg Forest, imagining Germany if the Romans had remained; at night he hears the wolves howl.

11 (Section XIII) Paderborn; a crucifix appears in the mist.

12 (Section IV, V) In a dream at Kyffhäuser, Heine sees Barbarossa, Roman Emperor and King of Germany, as a senile old man.

13 (Section XVI, XVII) Still at Kyffhäuser, Heine considers the guillotine, noose and sword as redundant for emperors now that the people rule.

14 (Section XVIII) At Minden, Heine is detained by the police.

15 (Section XIX) Heine visits his grandfather's birthplace at Buckeburg and meets Augustus I of Hanover.

16 (Section XX–XXVII) Heine finally arrives in Hamburg where he sees his mother, before walking around the city and meditating on how things can be and how they will end.

ONE HUNDRED YEARS OF SOLITUDE
FAMILY TREE

Colombian Gabriel García Márquez's novel was first published in Spanish in 1967, and has since been translated into more than 30 languages and sold over 20 million copies. This family tree offers a guide to the complex tale of six generations who are destined to repeat history.

Rebeca
Adopted orphan, marries José, eats earth

José Arcadio
First-born, enormous, covered in tattoos

Pilar Ternera

Santa Sofía de la Piedad
Wife of Arcadio, the transient, maternal member of the family

Arcadio
Proves a vicious dictator of Macondo during the uprising

Remedios the Beauty
Most beautiful woman in the world. Abruptly leaves the novel after floating to heaven

José Arcadio Segundo
Becomes a reclusive scholar; sole survivor of the massacre of the strikers against the banana company

Petra Cotes

Gaston
Husband of Amaranta Úrsula, travels to Belgium and never returns

Amarante Úrsula
Dies in childbirth when delivering the incestuous child of her nephew Aureliano (II)

José Arcadio Buendía
Patriarch, founder of Macondo

Úrsula Iguarán
Wife to José, lives to be 130

Colonel Aureliano Buendía
Second son, warrior, artist, father to 17 sons

RIP

Remedios Moscote
Wife to Colonel Buendía, dies during first pregnancy

Amaranta
Third child, dies a lonely spinster

Aureliano José
Obsessed with his aunt Amaranta

17 Aurelianos

Aureliano Segundo
Immense, boisterous and impulsive

Fernanda del Carpio
Strong religious views which she imposes

José Arcadio II - groomed to become Pope, slips into a life of debauchery after an unsuccessful trip to seminary

Meme - real name Renata Remedios, proves hedonistic like her father, lives out her life imprisoned in a convent after her affair with Mauricio

Aureliano II
Grows from a hermit to a scholar, and deciphers the prophecies of Melquíades. Fathers the last of the Buendía line with his aunt

Aureliano III
Incestuous child of Aureliano II and Amaranta Úrsula, who is born with the tail of a pig

AUSTEN VS **BRONTË**

Were Jane Austen and the Brontë sisters obsessed with bonnets, balls, dresses, marriage and matters of the heart? A search for key words in the collected novels of each show intriguing differences between works by the same authors.

NUMBER OF TIMES THAT WORD IS USED

TITLE

Sense and Sensibility

Pride and Prejudice

Mansfield Park

Emma

Northanger Abbey

Persuasion

Legend:
- X Bonnet
- X Ball
- X Dress
- X Heart
- X Darkness
- Marriage
- X Tears
- X Engagement
- X Love

NUMBER OF TIMES THAT WORD IS USED

TITLE

Jane Eyre

Shirley

Villette

Wuthering Heights

The Tenant of Wildfell Hall

Agnes Grey

STEAL THIS BOOK

Books get stolen from libraries – where you can take them away for free – and bookshops in their thousands every year. What gets stolen varies from city to city, place to place, but the libraries all seem to suffer from thieves with the same desires.

NEW YORK, USA BOOKSHOPS

TITLE	AUTHOR
All	Charles Bukowski
All	William Burroughs
On The Road	Jack Kerouac
The New York Trilogy	Paul Auster
All	Martin Amis
All	Jim Thompson
All	Philip K. Dick
All	Michel Foucault
All	Hunter S. Thompson
Graphic novels	Various

WORLD LIBRARIES

TITLE	AUTHOR	PLACE
The Bible	Various	
Wicca and witchcraft titles	Various	
Guinness World Records	Various	
Harry Potter (all)	J.K. Rowling	
Fifty Shades Of Grey (all)	E.L. James	
Exam prep guides	Various	
Art reference books	Various	
The Kama Sutra	Vatsyayana	
Business advice manuals	Various	
Swimsuit Annual	Sports Illustrated	

INTERNATIONAL SHOPLIFTING COSTS

TITLE	AUTHOR
USA	$41.7 billion
Japan	$9.6 billion
UK	$7.8 billion
Germany	$7.3 billion
France	$6.3 billion
Italy	$4.7 billion
Russia	$4 billion
Spain	$3.9 billion
Canada	$3.6 billion
Australia	$2 billion

LONDON, ENGLAND, BOOKSHOPS

TITLE	AUTHOR
London A–Z	Geographer's A–Z Map Co.
Lonely Planet Europe	Various
The Guv'nor	Lenny McLean
Tintin (all)	Hergé
Asterix (all)	Goscinny & Uderzo
Steal This Book	Abbie Hoffman
Spider-Man	Stan Lee
Wall And Piece	Banksy
Moleskin diaries (stationery)	n/a
The Virgin Suicides	Jeffrey Eugenides

SCOTLAND, BOOKSHOPS

TITLE	AUTHOR	PLACE
Harry Potter And The Chamber Of Secrets	J.K. Rowling	
Lovers And Players	Jackie Collins	
Diamond Girls	Jacqueline Wilson	
Rebus (all)	Ian Rankin	
DSA Driving Theory	HMSO	
Street Child	Berlie Doherty	
Charlie And The Chocolate Factory	Roald Dahl	
Discworld (all)	Terry Pratchett	
All	Stephen King	
All	Agatha Christie	

guardian.com, dailyrecord.com, huffingtonpost.com, publishersweekly.org, wikipedia

WOOD FOR **BOOKS**

Publishing isn't the greenest of industries, what with the vast majority of its key product being made of paper. Exactly how many trees each year get turned into books?

1 cord =
**15 trees OR
462 hardback
books w/200 pages**

1 cord of air-dried dense hardwood =
300 reams of paper

1 tree = **31 books**

At 31 books per tree that = **645 million trees in total each year to make books**

UNESCO calculates 2 million titles published annually with a varying print run =
2 billion books printed

Area of forested land per country
Most by PERCENTAGE

Suriname 94.6%
Sweden 68.7%
Japan 68.6%
Slovenia 62.3%
Republic of Korea 64%

Area of forested land per country
Most by SQ KM

Russian Federation 8.1M
USA 3M
China 2.1M
Sweden 0.3M—
Australia 1.5M

ecology.com, unesco.org, ehow.com, dataworldbank.org

THE MOST EXPENSIVE
RARE BOOKS

Rare books that command
a price in the millions of
dollars tend to be one-
off productions, often
handwritten and very old.

Handwritten

2007
The First Book Of Urizen
William Blake

Biblia Pauperum
Various
1460–1470

1794

Les Liliacées
Pierre-Joseph Redouté
1802

The Canterbury Tales
Geoffrey Chaucer
1476–1478

Traité Des Arbres Fruitiers
Henri-Louis Duhamel du Monceau
1768

St Cuthbert Gospel
Unknown
c7th

Don Quixote
Miguel De Cervantes
1605–1615

Geographia Cosmographia
Claudius Ptolemy
1478

The Gutenburg Bible
Various
1456

Birds Of America
John James Audubon
1827–1838

The Bay Psalm Book
Various
1640

De Humanis Corporis Fabrica
Andreas Vesalius
1543

Alice's Adventures
In Wonderland
1865 Lewis Carroll

The Rothschild Prayerbook
Unknown
1500–1520

First Folio
William Shakespeare
1623

The Gospels Of Henry The Lion
Order of St Benedict monks
c12th

De Revolutionibus Orbium Coelestium
Nicolaus Copernicus
1543

Magna Carta
Unknown
1297

The Codex Leicester
Leonardo da Vinci
C15th

600 ... 1100 1250 1300 1350 1400 1450 1500 1550 1600 1650 1700 1750 1800 1850 1900 1950 2000 2050

PUBLISHED

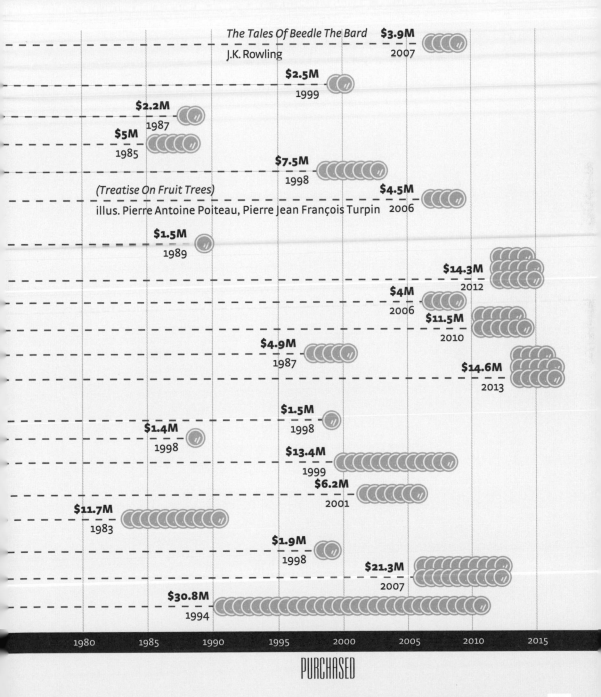

The Tales Of Beedle The Bard **$3.9M**
J.K. Rowling 2007

$2.5M
1999

$2.2M
1987

$5M
1985

$7.5M
1998

(Treatise On Fruit Trees) **$4.5M**
illus. Pierre Antoine Poiteau, Pierre Jean François Turpin 2006

$1.5M
1989

$14.3M
2012

$4M
2006

$11.5M
2010

$4.9M
1987

$14.6M
2013

$1.5M
1998

$1.4M
1998

$13.4M
1999

$6.2M
2001

$11.7M
1983

$1.9M
1998

$21.3M
2007

$30.8M
1994

1980   1985   1990   1995   2000   2005   2010   2015

PURCHASED

wikicollecting.org, 1stedition.net, abebooks.com, wikipedia.org

YOU **MUST** HAVE READ THIS...

The best-selling books in the world – excepting religious tomes – include some of the best-known novels of all time. Here are the books, some published many centuries ago, that have sold from tens to hundreds of millions of copies.

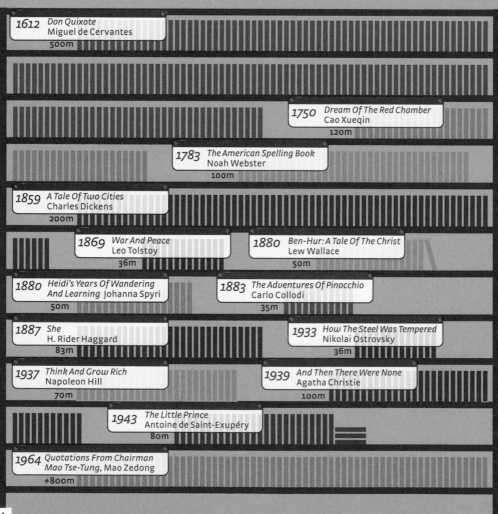

1612 *Don Quixote* Miguel de Cervantes
500m

1750 *Dream Of The Red Chamber* Cao Xueqin
120m

1783 *The American Spelling Book* Noah Webster
100m

1859 *A Tale Of Two Cities* Charles Dickens
200m

1869 *War And Peace* Leo Tolstoy
36m

1880 *Ben-Hur: A Tale Of The Christ* Lew Wallace
50m

1880 *Heidi's Years Of Wandering And Learning* Johanna Spyri
50m

1883 *The Adventures Of Pinocchio* Carlo Collodi
35m

1887 *She* H. Rider Haggard
83m

1933 *How The Steel Was Tempered* Nikolai Ostrovsky
36m

1937 *Think And Grow Rich* Napoleon Hill
70m

1939 *And Then There Were None* Agatha Christie
100m

1943 *The Little Prince* Antoine de Saint-Exupéry
80m

1964 *Quotations From Chairman Mao Tse-Tung*, Mao Zedong
+800m

| 1950 | The Lion, The Witch And The Wardrobe C.S. Lewis | | 1951 | The Catcher In The Rye J.D. Salinger |
85m

60m

| 1953 | Xinhua Zidian (dictionary) |
400m

| 1954 | The Lord Of The Rings J.R.R. Tolkien |
150m

| 1955 | Lolita Vladimir Nabokov | | 1980 | The Name Of The Rose Umberto Eco |
50m

50m

| 1988 | The Alchemist Paulo Coelho | | 1991 | Sophie's World Jostein Gaarder |
65m

40m

| 1997 | Harry Potter And The Sorcerer's Stone J.K. Rowling |
107m

| 1998 | Harry Potter And The Chamber Of Secrets J.K. Rowling | | 1999 | Harry Potter And The Prisoner Of Azkaban J.K. Rowling |
60m

50m

| 2000 | Harry Potter And The Goblet Of Fire J.K. Rowling | | 2003 | Harry Potter And The Order Of The Phoenix J.K. Rowling |
55m

55m

| 2003 | The Da Vinci Code Dan Brown | | 2005 | Harry Potter And The Half -Blood Prince J.K. Rowling |
80m

65m

| 2007 | Harry Potter And The Deathly Hallows J.K. Rowling |
45m

howstuffworks.com, wikipedia.org, huffingtonpost.com

THE ORIGINAL DHARMA **DRAMA**

The Indian epic poem The Ramayana *was written in 1000 BCE and remains one of the most read, interpreted and staged poems in the world. The story shares key aspects of plot with those of Homer, with families warring, wives abducted and gods in human form.*

JATAYU
Allied to Rama, a demi-god in the form of a vulture. Attempts to foil Ravana's kidnapping of Sita, gets his wings chopped off. Lives long enough to inform Rama.

SITA
Wife of Rama, incarnation of the Goddess of Wealth, Laxmi. Absolutely devoted to her husband, supremely chaste, willing to undergo test of fire to prove her purity. When driven into exile she is absorbed by Mother Earth.

HANUMAN
Allied to Rama, son of the God of Wind, Vayu, half-monkey half-man he has super strength and the ability to fly, and to grow to any size he wants. Carried a mountain on his back and set a city on fire using his tail as a torch.

DASHARATHA
Father and King of Ayodhya, undertook a ritual by the God of Fire so that his three wives would bear great progeny.

LAKSHMANA
Youngest son, loyal to Rama. Good with a bow and sword, great sidekick.

SRAMA
First-born son, incarnation of the god Vishnu. Embodies duty and honour (dharma). Destroyer of demons, possesses divine weaponry and super-strength. Reigned for 11,000 golden years, without war, calamity or disease. Weakness: the poison of a particular snake was said to put him into a coma.

VIBHISHANA
The demon brother of Ravana with a heart of gold. He urged Ravana to return Sita to her husband, and when Ravana refused, he sided with Rama's army and helped their victory. Was crowned the King of Lanka after Ravana's defeat and is a symbol of inherent good triumphing against all odds.

THE GOOD GUYS

SUGRIVA

Allied to Rama, son of the Sun God and King of the Vanars (Monkey-Men). Provided the army necessary for Rama to beat Ravana, after Ravana helped him defeat his brother and gain the throne.

KUMBHAKARANA

The brother of Ravana. A monstrously large demon who, by angering the gods, had the curse of sleeping for six months at a time, and waking for a single day where he would eat everything in sight. Woken by his brother on the eve of battle by having 1,000 elephants walk over him.

RAVANA

A great ruler, scholar, musician and devotee of the Lord Shiva. The symbol of greatness destroyed by base impulse. Has ten heads. Kidnapped Sita, Immortal and incapable of being defeated by even the gods, but neglected to ask for protection from the common man — as such, Rama was capable of vanquishing him.

THE BAD GUYS

INDRAJIT

The son of Ravana. A warrior, single-handedly destroyed the army of Sugriva. Killed by Lakshmana after a three day and night battle.

BHARATA

Second son, ruled while Rama was in exile — placed Rama's slippers on the throne, and sat on the step beneath it. Conquered vast amounts of land during his rule.

S

SURPANAKHA

Demoness sister of Ravana. Smitten by Rama and Lakshmana, and on attempting to seduce them, was rudely dismissed. Tried to assault Sita, Lakshmana cut off her nose. She urged Ravana to take Sita for his own. Said to be the ultimate catalyst of the Ramayana.

27

TAKE FOUR **DETECTIVES...**

Written by novelists from four different countries, all of whom have been best-sellers and made into television stars, mix and see what emerges.

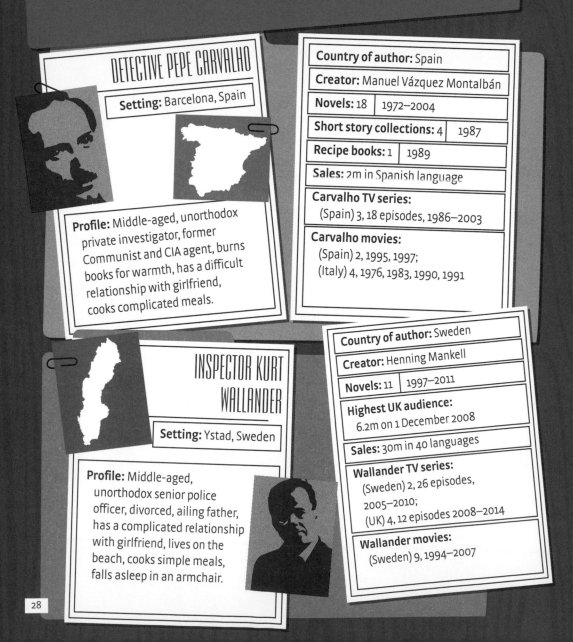

DETECTIVE PEPE CARVALHO

Setting: Barcelona, Spain

Profile: Middle-aged, unorthodox private investigator, former Communist and CIA agent, burns books for warmth, has a difficult relationship with girlfriend, cooks complicated meals.

Country of author: Spain

Creator: Manuel Vázquez Montalbán

| **Novels:** 18 | 1972–2004 |

| **Short story collections:** 4 | 1987 |

| **Recipe books:** 1 | 1989 |

Sales: 2m in Spanish language

Carvalho TV series:
 (Spain) 3, 18 episodes, 1986–2003

Carvalho movies:
 (Spain) 2, 1995, 1997;
 (Italy) 4, 1976, 1983, 1990, 1991

INSPECTOR KURT WALLANDER

Setting: Ystad, Sweden

Profile: Middle-aged, unorthodox senior police officer, divorced, ailing father, has a complicated relationship with girlfriend, lives on the beach, cooks simple meals, falls asleep in an armchair.

Country of author: Sweden

Creator: Henning Mankell

| **Novels:** 11 | 1997–2011 |

Highest UK audience:
 6.2m on 1 December 2008

Sales: 30m in 40 languages

Wallander TV series:
 (Sweden) 2, 26 episodes, 2005–2010;
 (UK) 4, 12 episodes 2008–2014

Wallander movies:
 (Sweden) 9, 1994–2007

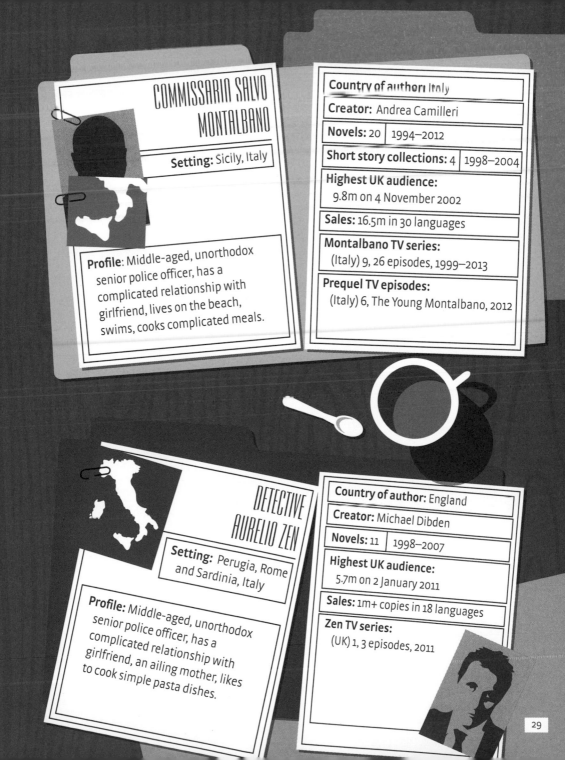

COMMISSARIO SALVO MONTALBANO

Setting: Sicily, Italy

Profile: Middle-aged, unorthodox senior police officer, has a complicated relationship with girlfriend, lives on the beach, swims, cooks complicated meals.

Country of author: Italy	
Creator: Andrea Camilleri	
Novels: 20	1994–2012
Short story collections: 4	1998–2004
Highest UK audience: 9.8m on 4 November 2002	
Sales: 16.5m in 30 languages	
Montalbano TV series: (Italy) 9, 26 episodes, 1999–2013	
Prequel TV episodes: (Italy) 6, The Young Montalbano, 2012	

DETECTIVE AURELIO ZEN

Setting: Perugia, Rome and Sardinia, Italy

Profile: Middle-aged, unorthodox senior police officer, has a complicated relationship with girlfriend, an ailing mother, likes to cook simple pasta dishes.

Country of author: England	
Creator: Michael Dibden	
Novels: 11	1998–2007
Highest UK audience: 5.7m on 2 January 2011	
Sales: 1m+ copies in 18 languages	
Zen TV series: (UK) 1, 3 episodes, 2011	

GIVING UP THE **DAY JOB**

Writers become professional when they have sold enough books to be able to guarantee that the bills will be paid, so they write in their spare time, while working at a 'day job'. Here's what several successful authors would have been earning if they'd continued with their first occupation, and what they or their estate is worth now.

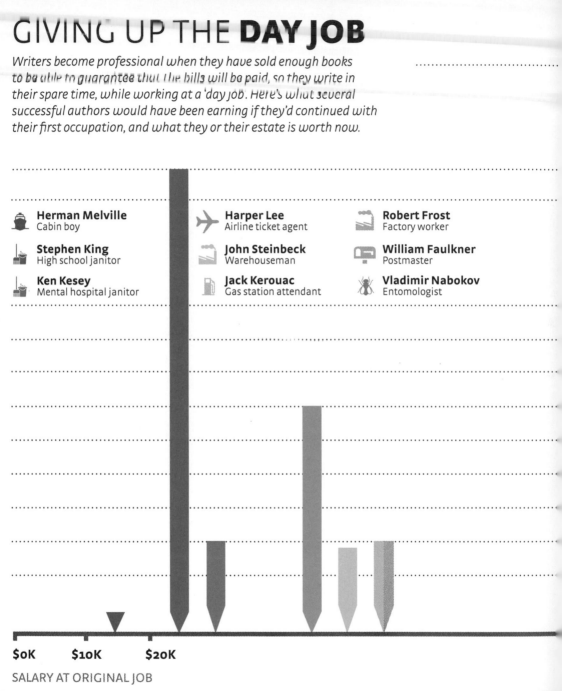

Herman Melville
Cabin boy

Stephen King
High school janitor

Ken Kesey
Mental hospital janitor

Harper Lee
Airline ticket agent

John Steinbeck
Warehouseman

Jack Kerouac
Gas station attendant

Robert Frost
Factory worker

William Faulkner
Postmaster

Vladimir Nabokov
Entomologist

$0K $10K $20K

SALARY AT ORIGINAL JOB

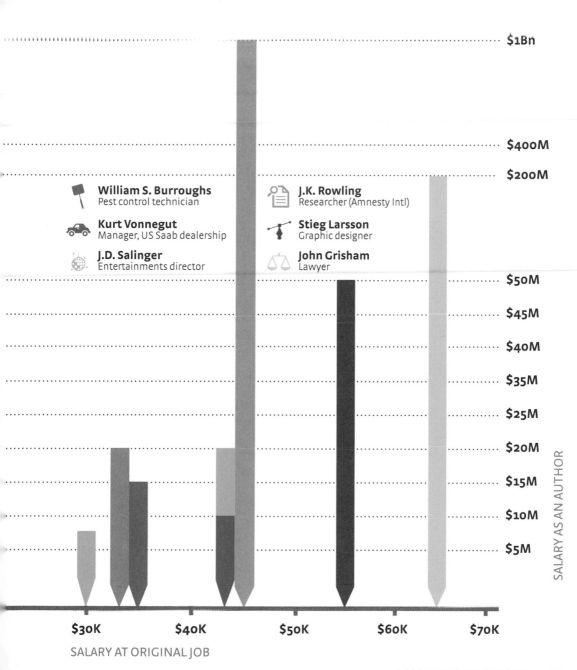

$1Bn

$400M

$200M

William S. Burroughs
Pest control technician

J.K. Rowling
Researcher (Amnesty Intl)

Kurt Vonnegut
Manager, US Saab dealership

Stieg Larsson
Graphic designer

J.D. Salinger
Entertainments director

John Grisham
Lawyer

$50M

$45M

$40M

$35M

$25M

$20M

$15M

$10M

$5M

SALARY AS AN AUTHOR

$30K $40K $50K $60K $70K

SALARY AT ORIGINAL JOB

MOTHER DEAREST?

Family matters are a major theme in the great novels of the 19th and early 20th centuries. From Jane Austen to Virginia Woolf, via Charles Dickens, George Eliot, Oscar Wilde, D.H. Lawrence and E.M. Forster, the role of the mother was minutely examined and often found wanting. Here's how the mothers in the major works of each author measure up, as either good, bad, or simply dead.

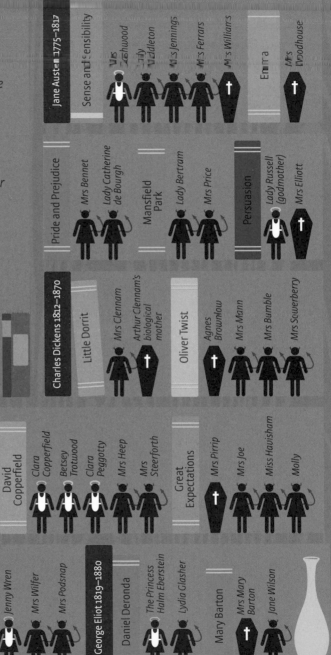

Jane Austen 1775–1817

Sense and Sensibility — Mrs Dashwood, Lady Middleton, Mrs Jennings, Mrs Ferrars, Emma, Mrs Woodhouse

Pride and Prejudice — Mrs Bennet, Lady Catherine de Bourgh

Mansfield Park — Lady Bertram, Mrs Price

Persuasion — Lady Russell (godmother), Mrs Elliott

Charles Dickens 1812–1870

Little Dorrit — Mrs Clennam, Arthur Clennam's biological mother

Oliver Twist — Agnes Brownlow, Mrs Mann, Mrs Bumble, Mrs Sowerberry

The Old Curiosity Shop — Mrs Trent

Nicholas Nickleby — Mrs Nickleby, Mrs Squeers, Mrs Witterly

David Copperfield — Clara Copperfield, Betsey Trotwood, Clara Peggotty, Mrs Heep, Mrs Steerforth

Great Expectations — Mrs Pirrip, Mrs Joe, Miss Havisham, Molly

Bleak House — Honoria, Lady Dedlock, Mrs Barbary, Mrs Jellyby

Our Mutual Friend — Mrs Henrietta Boffin, Jenny Wren, Mrs Wilfer, Mrs Podsnap

George Eliot 1819–1880

Daniel Deronda — The Princess Halm Eberstein, Lydia Glasher

Mary Barton — Mrs Mary Barton, Jane Wilson

Oscar Wilde 1854–1900

The Importance Of Being Earnest — *Lady Bracknell*

Salome — *Herodias*

A Woman Of No Importance — *Mrs Arbuthnot*

Lady Windermere's Fan — *Mrs Erlynne*

E.M. Forster 1879–1970

A Passage To India — *Mrs Moore*

Where Angels Fear To Tread — *Lilia Herriton*

A Room With A View — *Mrs Honeychurch*

Howards End — *Ruth Wilcox*

The Other Boat — *Mrs March*

The Longest Journey — *Mrs Elliot*

D.H. Lawrence 1885–1930

Sons And Lovers — *Mrs Morel*

Odour Of Chrysanthemums — *Elizabeth Bates* / *Walter's mother*

The Rocking Horse Winner — *Hester*

The Virgin And The Gypsy — *Mater*

Virginia Woolf 1882–1941

Mrs Dalloway — *Clarissa Dalloway*

To The Lighthouse — *Mrs Ramsay*

Night And Day — *Margaret Hilbery*

The Voyage Out — *Helen Ambrose*

Albert Camus 1913–1960

The Stranger — *Mme Mersault* †

The Plague — *Mme Rieux*

The Fall — *various widows with orphans*

A Happy Death — *Mme Mersault* †

The First Man — *Catherine Cormery*

BANNED
BOOKS

Since even before Gutenberg set his first press, books have been banned in different countries and for different reasons. From the 8th to the

REASON WHY

HOMOSEXUAL CONTENT
HELIOCENTRIC HERESY
SEXUAL OBSCENITY

HERETICAL

PRO-DEMOCRATIC

OBSCENITY

DEPRAVED, IMMORAL, PSYCHOTIC, VULGAR, ANTI-CHRISTIAN
RACIALLY OFFENSIVE
LIBELLOUS, PRO- COMMUNIST
PRO- COMMUNIST
SEX, OBSCENITY
PROFANITY
OFFENSIVE LANGUAGE
VIOLENCE
ENCOURAGING PROMISCUITY
ANTI-COMMUNIST
GLORIFYING ROYAL FAMILIES
INCLUSION OF TALKING PIGS
CRITICISM OF GOVERNMENT
ANTHROPOMORPHIC ANIMALS

ANTI-ISLAMIC/ OFFENSIVE TO ISLAM

OFFENSIVE TO ISLAM

TITLE AND WRITER

Poetry On Love And Family, Sappho ■
Dialogue Concerning The Two Chief World Systems, Galileo Galilei ■
The Hunchback of Notre-Dame, Victor Hugo ■
The Bible, Various/Martin Luther ■
Paradise Lost, John Milton ■
Tyndale Bible, Various/John Tyndale ■
Maya Codices, Various ■
The Talmud, Various ■
The Odyssey, Homer ■

Lolita, Vladimir Nabokov

Ars Amatoria, Ovid

Ulysses, James Joyce ■
Lady Chatterley's Lover, D.H. Lawrence ■

The Color Purple, Alice Walker ■

Howl, Alan Ginsberg ■
Huckleberry Finn, Mark Twain ■

Slaughterhouse-Five, Kurt Vonnegut ■

The Grapes Of Wrath, John Steinbeck ■
American Psycho, Bret Easton Ellis ■
The Catcher In The Rye, J.D. Salinger ■
I Know Why The Caged Bird Sings, Maya Angelou ■
Bridge To Terabithia, Katherine Paterson ■
Catch-22, Joseph Heller ■
The Adventures Of Captain Underpants, Dav Pilkey ■
Brave New World, Aldous Huxley ■
Animal Farm, George Orwell ■
Fairy Tales, Hans Christian Andersen ■
Alice's Adventures In Wonderland, Lewis Carroll ■

The Satanic Verses, Salman Rushdie

Harry Potter series, J.K. Rowling ■

21st centuries, here are the 30 most infamous
— and sometimes surprising — books to have
been banned from public consumption

WHERE BANNED:
Christian Church
England
Mexico
France
Roman Empire
Argentina
New Zealand
South Africa
Canada
UK
Florence, Italy
USA
Australia
Ireland
USSR
China
Kenya
Bangladesh
India
Pakistan
Iran
Egypt
Kuwait
Tanzania
Liberia
Malaysia
Sri Lanka
Papua New Guinea
Senegal
Singapore
Thailand
United Arab Emirates

WHEN BANNED:
AD 5 & 1073
1633
1834
1624
1758
1525
16th century
1225
AD 35
AD 8
1955
1921
1497
1928
1986 & 1999
1992
1997
1957
1885
1996
1973
1972
1982
2011
1939
1978
1983–2012
1986
2012
1991
1932
1835
1930
1945
1931
1988
2002

WHERE BANNED   WHEN BANNED

ala.org, oif.ala.org, bannedbooks.world.edu, wikipedia.org

THE WORLDS OF **CLOUD ATLAS**

David Mitchell's acclaimed 2004 novel takes the reader through six different stories that occur in different times, places and even worlds. The first five stories build to the middle section of the story and then each in turn unfold as the book draws to a close. Here's how all are linked.

'THERE IS A NATURAL ORDER TO THIS WORLD, AND THOSE WHO TRY TO UPEND IT DO NOT FARE WELL'

FEAR

MYTHOLOGY

MENTAL SLAVERY

SLAVERY

CARNIVORISM

CONSUMERISM

GERONTOPHOBIA

ABUSE

POWER

EARTH EXPLOITATION

SEXISM

HOMOPHOBIA

PREJUDICE

SLAVERY

DECEPTION

'TRUTH IS SINGULAR. ITS VERSIONS ARE MISTRUTHS'

THE REVELATION OF SONMI-451
recorded by Archivist Park

SONMI-451 ORISON

ZACHRY

SONMI-451

'THE GHASTLY ORDEAL OF TIMOTHY CAVENDISH'

HALF LIVES: A LUISA REY MYSTERY
by Javier Gomez

TIMOTHY CAVENDISH

THE HYDRA FACTOR REPORT

LUISA

LETTERS TO SIXSMITH

THE CLOUD ATLAS SEXTET
by Robert Frobisher

ROBERT FROBISHER

THE PACIFIC JOURNAL
by Adam Ewing

ADAM EWING

ZACHRY'S TALE

37

WAR AND PEACE

Prince Nikolai Bolkonsky

Andrei

Natasha

Mitya (Dimitriy)

Lisa Karlovna Bolkonskaya née Meinena + Prince Andrei Nikolayevich Bolkonsky

Princess Marya Bolkonskaya + Count Nicolai Rostov

Sonya (surname unknown)

Petya Rostova

Vera Rostova + Alphonse Karlovich Berg

Late Princess Bolkonskaya + Old Prince Nikolai Bolkonsky

Alexander (surname unknown)

Old Count Ilya Rostov + Old Countess Natalya Rostova

Count Pyotr Nikolaitch Shinshin

Pyotr's married brother + Pyotr's cousin

Andrei Rostov's brother or sister

Andrei Rostov

Count Shinshin

Nikolai Shinshin

Nikolai Shinshin's brother or sister

Count Rostov

Count Shinshin

BOLKONSKY FAMILY

ROSTOV FAMILY

SHINSHIN FAMILY

Tolstoy's enormous novel was first published in 1869 in a first edition
that ran to 1,225 pages. It has since become the most admired, if least-
read, popular book of all time. Here's a handy guide to the family trees of
the seven families around whom the plot turns for you to refer to.

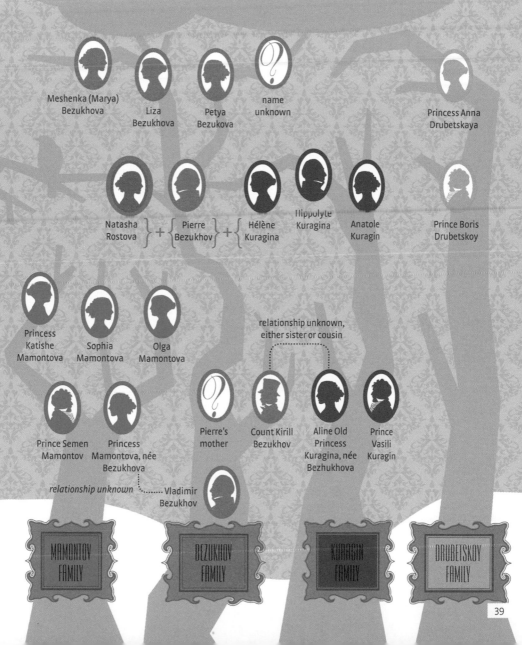

Meshenka (Marya)
Bezukhova

Liza
Bezukhova

Petya
Bezukova

name
unknown

Princess Anna
Drubetskaya

Natasha
Rostova } + { Pierre
Bezukhov } + { Hélène
Kuragina

Hippolyte
Kuragina

Anatole
Kuragin

Prince Boris
Drubetskoy

Princess
Katishe
Mamontova

Sophia
Mamontova

Olga
Mamontova

relationship unknown,
either sister or cousin

Prince Semen
Mamontov

Princess
Mamontova, née
Bezukhova

Pierre's
mother

Count Kirill
Bezukhov

Aline Old
Princess
Kuragina, née
Bezhukhova

Prince
Vasili
Kuragin

relationship unknown ········ Vladimir
Bezukhov

MAMONTOV
FAMILY

BEZUKHOV
FAMILY

KURAGIN
FAMILY

DRUBETSKOY
FAMILY

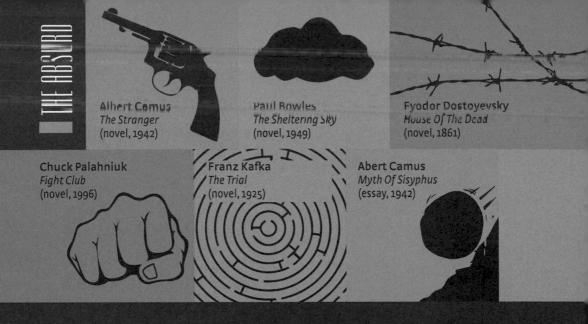

Albert Camus
The Stranger
(novel, 1942)

Paul Bowles
The Sheltering Sky
(novel, 1949)

Fyodor Dostoyevsky
House Of The Dead
(novel, 1861)

Chuck Palahniuk
Fight Club
(novel, 1996)

Franz Kafka
The Trial
(novel, 1925)

Abert Camus
Myth Of Sisyphus
(essay, 1942)

EXISTENTIAL SYMBOLS

*The great existential writers of the world used symbolic objects in their work
to demonstrate aspects of the absurd, nihilism, despair and alienation. This
visual guide explains who used what, when and what they represent.*

Samuel Beckett
Waiting For Godot
(play, 1953)

Kurt Vonnegut
Slaughterhouse-Five
(novel, 1969)

Albert Camus
Caligula
(play, 1939)

Kobo Abe
The Woman In The Dunes
(novel, 1962)

Paul Celan
Poppy And Memory
(poem, 1952)

Samuel Beckett
Endgame
(play, 1957)

Franz Kafka
The Metamorphosis
(novella, 1915)

Joseph Conrad
The Heart Of Darkness
(novel, 1899)

Fyodor Dostoyevsky
Crime And Punishment
(novel, 1866)

Jean-Paul Sartre
Nausea
(novel, 1938)

Ivan Turgenev
Fathers And Sons
(novel, 1862)

Eugène Ionesco
Rhinoceros
(play, 1959)

ALIENATION

Eugène Ionesco
The New Tenant
(play, 1955)

T.S. Eliot
The Hollow Men
(poem, 1925)

Jean-Paul Sartre
No Exit
(play, 1944)

Hermann Hesse
Steppenwolf
(novel, 1927)

William Faulkner
As I Lay Dying
(novel, 1930)

Edward Albee
Who's Afraid Of Virginia Woolf?
(play, 1962)

DESPAIR

Tom Stoppard
Rosencrantz And Guildenstern Are Dead
(play, 1966)

William Shakespeare
Hamlet
(play, 1599–1602)

Ralph Ellison
Invisible Man
(novel, 1952)

41

SHAKESPEARE **ETERNAL**

The plays of William Shakespeare have proven to be the inspiration, starting point and whole context for countless rewrites. These six plays have inspired a strange bunch of versions in different modern publishing genres.

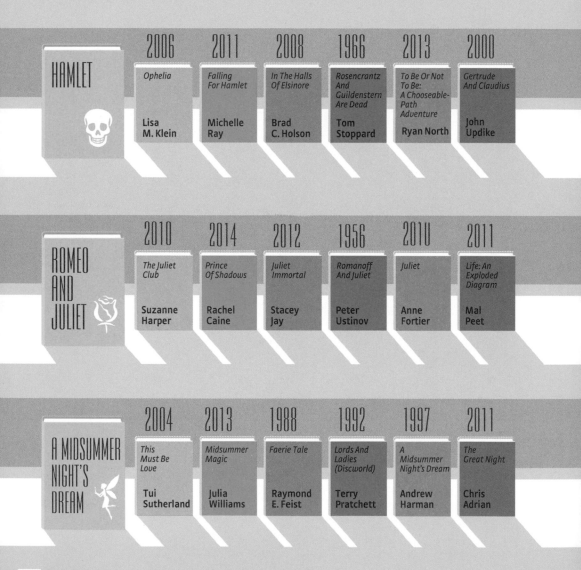

HAMLET

2006	2011	2008	1966	2013	2000
Ophelia	Falling For Hamlet	In The Halls Of Elsinore	Rosencrantz And Guildenstern Are Dead	To Be Or Not To Be: A Chooseable-Path Adventure	Gertrude And Claudius
Lisa M. Klein	Michelle Ray	Brad C. Holson	Tom Stoppard	Ryan North	John Updike

ROMEO AND JULIET

2010	2014	2012	1956	2010	2011
The Juliet Club	Prince Of Shadows	Juliet Immortal	Romanoff And Juliet	Juliet	Life: An Exploded Diagram
Suzanne Harper	Rachel Caine	Stacey Jay	Peter Ustinov	Anne Fortier	Mal Peet

A MIDSUMMER NIGHT'S DREAM

2004	2013	1988	1992	1997	2011
This Must Be Love	Midsummer Magic	Faerie Tale	Lords And Ladies (Discworld)	A Midsummer Night's Dream	The Great Night
Tui Sutherland	Julia Williams	Raymond E. Feist	Terry Pratchett	Andrew Harman	Chris Adrian

	YOUNG ADULT	CHICK LIT	HORROR	COMEDY	ACTION/ ADVENTURE	LITERARY FICTION
THE TEMPEST	2013 *Undine* Penni Russon	2010 *The Gentleman Poet *)* Kathryn Johnson	2010 *Prospero Lost* L. Jagi Lamplighter	2012 *Tempestuous (Twisted Lit)* Askew & Helmes	2010 *The Dream Of Perpetual Motion* Dexter Palmer	1989 *Mama Day* Gloria Naylor

* The Gentleman Poet: A Novel Of Love, Danger, And Shakespeare's The Tempest

MACBETH	2007 *Enter Three Witches* Caroline B. Cooney	2008 *Lady MacBeth: A Novel* Susan Fraser King	2008 *The Lost Kings* Andrew Reimann	1980 *Wyrd Sisters (Discworld)* Terry Pratchett	1982 *Light Thickens* Naigo Marsh	1973 *Macbett* Eugene Ionesco

THE MERCHANT OF VENICE	2001 *Shylock's Daughter* Mirjam Pressler	2004 *Shylock's Daughter: A Novel Of Love In Venice* Erica Jong	2008 *The Merchant Of Venice* Gareth Hinds	2014 *The Serpent Of Venice: A Novel* Christopher Moore	2003 *The Merchant Of Vengeance* Simon Hawke	1994 *Operation Shylock: A Confession* Philip Roth

THE SHAPES OF STORIES ACCORDING TO
KURT VONNEGUT

MAN IN HOLE

The main character gets into trouble, then gets out of it again, and ends up better off for the experience.

Arsenic and Old Lace

Harold & Kumar Go To White Castle

BOY MEETS GIRL

The main character comes across something wonderful, gets it, loses it, then gets it back forever.

Jane Eyre

Eternal Sunshine Of The Spotless Mind

FROM BAD TO WORSE

The main character starts off poorly then gets continually worse with no hope for improvement.

The Metamorphosis

The Twilight Zone

WHICH WAY IS UP?

The story has a lifelike ambiguity that keeps us from knowing if new developments are good or bad.

Hamlet

The Sopranos

Kurt Vonnegut gained worldwide fame and adoration through the publication of his novels, including Slaughterhouse-Five, Cat's Cradle, Breakfast Of Champions, and more. But it was his rejected master's thesis in anthropology that he called his prettiest contribution to culture. The basic idea of his thesis was that a story's main character has ups and downs that can be graphed to reveal the story's shape. The shape of a society's stories, he said, is at least as interesting as the shape of its pots or spearheads. Let's have a look.

CREATION STORY

In many cultures' creation stories, humankind receives incremental gifts from a deity. First, major staples like the earth and sky, then smaller things like sparrows and cell phones. Not a common shape for Western stories, however.

OLD TESTAMENT

Humankind receives incremental gifts from a deity, but is suddenly ousted from good standing in a fall of enormous proportions.

Great Expectations with original ending

NEW TESTAMENT

Humankind receives incremental gifts from a deity, is suddenly ousted from good standing, but then receives off-the-charts bliss.

 Great Expectations with revised ending

CINDERELLA

It was the similarity between the shapes of *Cinderella* and the *New Testament* that thrilled Vonnegut for the first time in 1947, and then over the course of his life as he continued to write essays and give lectures on the shapes of stories.

A Man Without A Country and Palm Sunday by Kurt Vonnegut

REFERENCES **REQUIRED**

Writers are often inspired by other writers. If it's not Shakespeare then it's usually another great from the canon of literary history. However, there are now works of fiction that are considered a part of the canon that were inspired by earlier, lesser-known works.

NEW WORK

Vanity Fair novel by William Makepeace Thackeray — **1847**

Far From The Madding Crowd novel by Thomas Hardy — **1874**

A Passage To India novel by E.M. Forster — **1924**

As I Lay Dying novel by William Faulkner — **1930**

Tender Is the Night novel by F. Scott Fitzgerald — **1932**

Of Mice And Men novella by John Steinbeck — **1937**

Blithe Spirit play by Noël Coward — **1941**

Things Fall Apart novel by Chinua Achebe — **1958**

Mother Night novel by Kurt Vonnegut — **1961**

I Know Why The Caged Bird Sings autobiography by Maya Angelou — **1969**

A Confederacy Of Dunces novel by John Kennedy Toole — **1980**

His Dark Materials trilogy by Philip Pullman — **1995–2000**

Everything Is Illuminated novel by Jonathan Safran Foer — **2002**

The Curious Incident Of The Dog In The Night-Time novel by Mark Haddon — **2003**

No Country For Old Men novel by Cormac McCarthy — **2005**

OLD WORK

c.7–8th century – *The Odyssey* epic poem by Homer

1667 – *Paradise Lost* epic poem by John Milton

1678 – *The Pilgrim's Progress* work by John Bunyan

1703 – *Thoughts On Various Subjects, Moral And Diverting* essay by Jonathan Swift

1751 – *Elegy Written In A Country Churchyard* poem by Thomas Gray

1785 – *To A Mouse* poem by Robert Burns

1808 – *Faust Part One* play by Johann Wolfgang von Goethe

1819 – *Ode To A Nightingale* poem by John Keats

1820 – *To A Skylark* poem by Percy Bysshe Shelley

1855 – Walt Whitman's poem of the same name

1892 – *Silver Blaze* Sherlock Holmes story by Arthur Conan Doyle

1899 – *Sympathy* poem by Paul Laurence Dunbar

1919 – *The Second Coming* poem by W.B. Yeats

1926 – *Sailing To Byzantium* poem by W.B. Yeats

1984 – *The Unbearable Lightness Of Being* novel by Milan Kundera

THE BLOOMSBURY
GROUP NETWORK

They were the most infamous, ingenious and interrelated group of writers, critics, artists and publishers in London in the early 20th century, and helped define and promote modernism in literature. Here's who they were, what they did, and with whom.

Clive Bell
Art Critic

Vanessa Bell
Post-Impressionist Painter

E.M. Forster
Novelist

Roger Fry
Art Critic and
Post-Impressionist Painter

Duncan Grant
Post-Impressionist
Painter

Roger Fry, Vanessa Bell and Duncan Grant collaborated
on the Omega Workshops design enterprise

Vanessa Bell painted portraits of Virginia Woolf and David Garnett

Quentin Bell wrote biography of Virginia Woolf

Vita Sackville-West
Novelist

David Garnett
Writer and Publisher

Angelica Garnett
Writer and Painter
daughter of Vanessa Bell and
Duncan Grant (raised as Clive Bell's)

sons of Vanessa Bell and Clive Bell

Quentin Bell
Art Historian and Author

Julian Bell
Poet

Studied together at Cambridge Siblings Cousins Lovers

Marriages Parents/Children Artistic collaborations

John Maynard Keynes
Economist

Desmond MacCarthy
Literary Journalist

Lytton Strachey
Biographer

James Strachey
Psychoanalyst

Leonard Woolf
Essayist and Novelist

Leonard Woolf and Virginia Woolf founded the Hogarth Press, which published work by Virginia Woolf, Vanessa Bell and Vita Sackville-West

Virginia Woolf wrote biography of Roger Fry

Mary (Molly) MacCarthy
Novelist

Saxon Sydney-Turner
Civil Servant

Karin Stephen
Psychoanalyst and Psychologist

Adrian Stephen
Author and Psychoanalyst

Virginia Woolf
Novelist

WRITER'S **REST**

Here are the sleeping and writing patterns of more than a dozen of the world's most famous authors.

hours writing

HOURS SPENT WRITING

Jane Austen (1775–1817)	5
Anthony Trollope (1815–1882)	3
Jean-Paul Sartre (1905–1980)	6
Simone de Beauvoir (1908–1986)	7
Saul Bellow (1915–2005)	4
Kingsley Amis (1922–1995)	9

Maya Angelou (1928–)	7
John Updike (1932–2009)	3.5
Philip Roth (1933–)	8
Joyce Carol Oates (1938–)	8
Stephen King (1947–)	4
David Foster Wallace (1962–2008)	3

HOURS SPENT WRITING/SLEEPING

	✎	☾		✎	☾
Honoré de Balzac (1799–1850)	13.5	7.5	Vladimir Nabokov (1899–1977)	11.5	10
Charles Dickens (1812–1870)	5	7	Georges Simenon (1903–1989)	3	8
Gustave Flaubert (1821–1880)	5	7	W.H. Auden (1907–1973)	8.5	8.5
Gertrude Stein (1874–1946)	0.5	7	Flannery O'Connor (1925–1964)	3	9
Thomas Mann (1875–1955)	3	8	William Styron (1925–2006)	4	9
Franz Kafka (1883–1924)	3	8.5	Haruki Murakami (1949–)	5	7
F. Scott Fitzgerald (1896–1940)	10.5	7			

Daily Rituals: How Great Minds Make Time, Find Inspiration, and Get to Work by Mason Currey (Picador, 2013) 51

IN THE LAP OF **THE GODS**

The works of Homer, Hesiod, Sophocles and other ancient Greek writers are filled with the names and deeds of the gods who ruled the world. This is a who's who of the first tier of Greek gods and goddesses, their symbols, patronage and family tree.

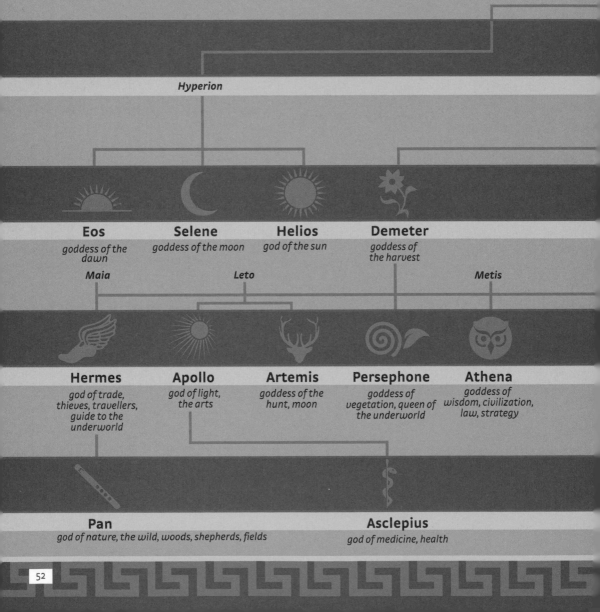

Hyperion

Eos
goddess of the dawn

Selene
goddess of the moon

Helios
god of the sun

Demeter
goddess of the harvest

Maia

Leto

Metis

Hermes
god of trade, thieves, travellers, guide to the underworld

Apollo
god of light, the arts

Artemis
goddess of the hunt, moon

Persephone
goddess of vegetation, queen of the underworld

Athena
goddess of wisdom, civilization, law, strategy

Pan
god of nature, the wild, woods, shepherds, fields

Asclepius
god of medicine, health

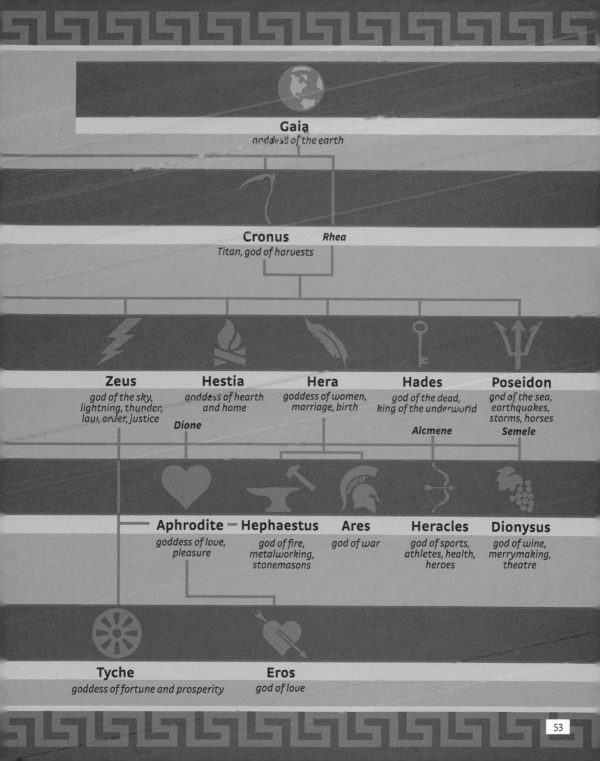

Gaia
goddess of the earth

Cronus   *Rhea*
Titan, god of harvests

Zeus
*god of the sky,
lightning, thunder,
law, order, justice*

Hestia
*goddess of hearth
and home*

Hera
*goddess of women,
marriage, birth*

Hades
*god of the dead,
king of the underworld*

Poseidon
*god of the sea,
earthquakes,
storms, horses*

Dione

Alcmene

Semele

Aphrodite — **Hephaestus**
*goddess of love,
pleasure*

Hephaestus
*god of fire,
metalworking,
stonemasons*

Ares
god of war

Heracles
*god of sports,
athletes, health,
heroes*

Dionysus
*god of wine,
merrymaking,
theatre*

Tyche
goddess of fortune and prosperity

Eros
god of love

DUCK **OR** SEAGULL?

The social dramas of Norwegian playwright Henrik Ibsen (1828–1906) and Russian Anton Chekhov (1860–1904) changed the shape and concerns of theatre in the 20th century. Their works had a lot in common, as this examination of four of the best known and most popular plays by each man demonstrates.

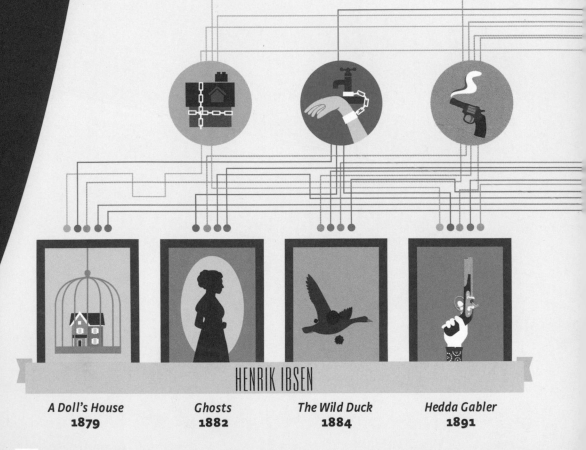

HENRIK IBSEN

| *A Doll's House* | *Ghosts* | *The Wild Duck* | *Hedda Gabler* |
| **1879** | **1882** | **1884** | **1891** |

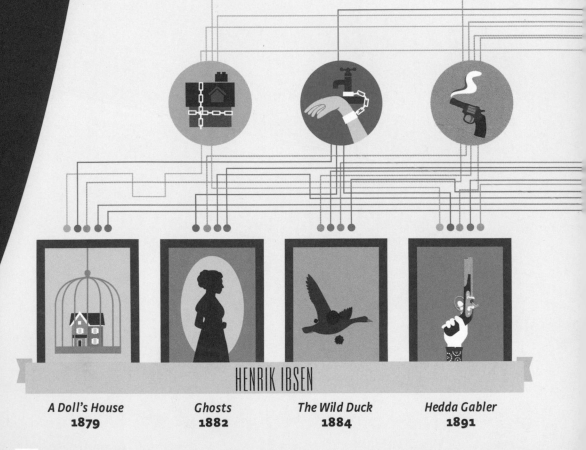

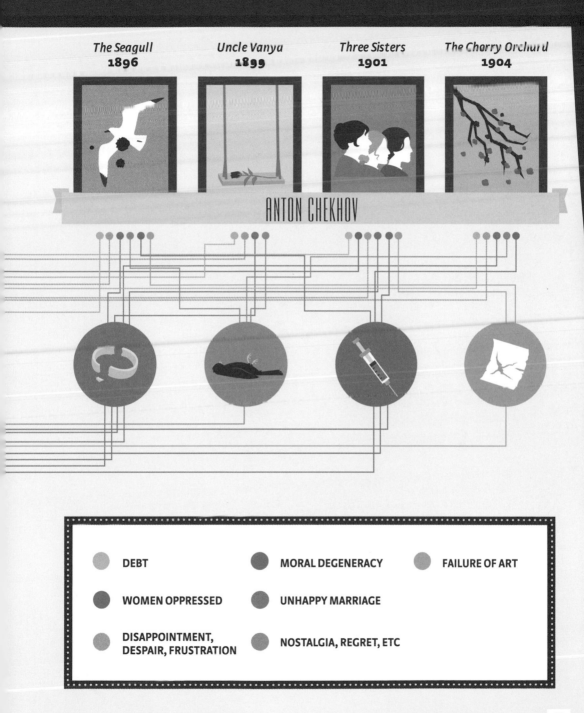

The Seagull 1896

Uncle Vanya 1899

Three Sisters 1901

The Cherry Orchard 1904

ANTON CHEKHOV

DEBT

MORAL DEGENERACY

FAILURE OF ART

WOMEN OPPRESSED

UNHAPPY MARRIAGE

DISAPPOINTMENT, DESPAIR, FRUSTRATION

NOSTALGIA, REGRET, ETC

MEET ME IN **PARIS**

Imagining the literary characters of different centuries and authors meeting at the great locations of Paris where their stories are set.

(H) Hotel Ritz, Place Vendôme
Head waiter meets bartender

Aime from Marcel Proust's *In Search Of Lost Time*
meets
Alix from F. Scott Fitzgerald's *Babylon Revisited*

(K) Arc de Triomphe
Idealistic nobleman meets misanthropic nobleman

D'Artagnan from Alexandre Dumas' *The Three Musketeers*
meets
Alceste from Molière's *The Misanthrope*

(B) The Right Bank, Palais Royale
Traitorous poet meets gullible businessman

Lucien de Rubempré from Honoré de Balzac's *Lost Illusions*
meets
Christopher Newman from Henry James' *The American*

(C) Left Bank, The Latin Quarter
Impotent journalist meets runaway stockbroker

Jake Barnes from Ernest Hemingway's *The Sun Also Rises*
meets
Charles Strickland from Somerset Maugham's *The Moon And Sixpence*

(G) Boulevard Saint-Germaine, Cafe Flor
Existentialist meets individual

Mathieu from Jean-Paul Sartre's *The Age Of Reason*
meets
Jean from Simone de Beauvoir's *Blood Of Others*

(F) Sorbonne District
Bored law student meets unstable middle-aged housewife

Dominique from Françoise Sagan's *A Certain Smile*
meets
Sasha Jensen from Jean Rhys' *Good Morning Midnight*

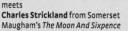

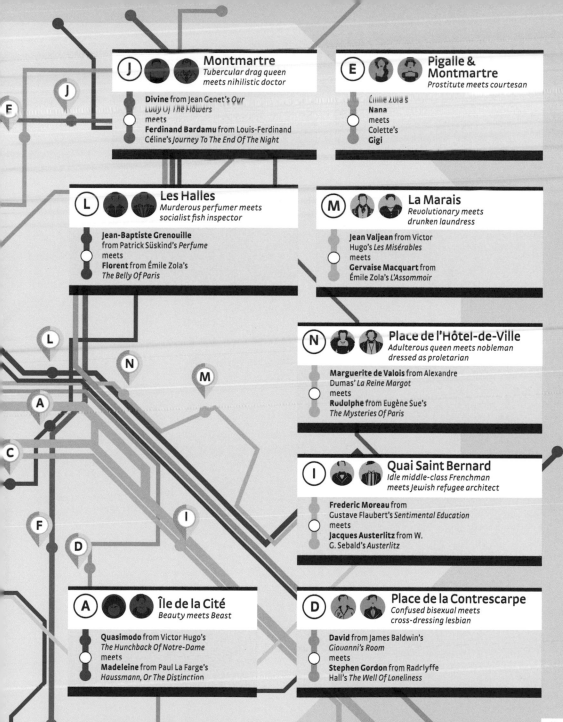

J — **Montmartre**
Tubercular drag queen meets nihilistic doctor

Divine from Jean Genet's *Our Lady Of The Flowers*
meets
Ferdinand Bardamu from Louis-Ferdinand Céline's *Journey To The End Of The Night*

E — **Pigalle & Montmartre**
Prostitute meets courtesan

Émile Zola's **Nana**
meets
Colette's **Gigi**

L — **Les Halles**
Murderous perfumer meets socialist fish inspector

Jean-Baptiste Grenouille from Patrick Süskind's *Perfume*
meets
Florent from Émile Zola's *The Belly Of Paris*

M — **La Marais**
Revolutionary meets drunken laundress

Jean Valjean from Victor Hugo's *Les Misérables*
meets
Gervaise Macquart from Émile Zola's *L'Assommoir*

N — **Place de l'Hôtel-de-Ville**
Adulterous queen meets nobleman dressed as proletarian

Marguerite de Valois from Alexandre Dumas' *La Reine Margot*
meets
Rudolphe from Eugène Sue's *The Mysteries Of Paris*

I — **Quai Saint Bernard**
Idle middle-class Frenchman meets Jewish refugee architect

Frederic Moreau from Gustave Flaubert's *Sentimental Education*
meets
Jacques Austerlitz from W. G. Sebald's *Austerlitz*

A — **Île de la Cité**
Beauty meets Beast

Quasimodo from Victor Hugo's *The Hunchback Of Notre-Dame*
meets
Madeleine from Paul La Farge's *Haussmann, Or The Distinction*

D — **Place de la Contrescarpe**
Confused bisexual meets cross-dressing lesbian

David from James Baldwin's *Giovanni's Room*
meets
Stephen Gordon from Radclyffe Hall's *The Well Of Loneliness*

THE **FINAL** CHAPTER

In death, as so often in life, truth is stranger than fiction. And it is predominantly novelists, poets and playwrights who have met with sad and terrible deaths, as these famous examples from around the world show.

Suicide

Death stranger than fiction

Murder

ALBERT CAMUS
novelist
{ d. 4 January 1960, Villeblevin, Burgundy, France }

Car crashed into a tree on a straight road on a bright day, no other vehicles involved. Aged 46.

JOHN KENNEDY TOOLE
novelist
{ d. 26 March 1969, Biloxi MSS, USA }

Gassed by car exhaust fumes. Aged 31.

DONALD GOINES
(A.K.A. Al C. Clark)
novelist
{ d. 21 October 1974, Detroit MI, USA }

Gunshot wounds, unknown assailant. Aged 37.

ROLAND BARTHES
literary critic
{ d. 25 February 1980, Paris, France }

Hit by a laundry van while crossing the road. Aged 64.

BRUNO SCHULZ
novelist
{ d. 19 November 1942, Drohobych, Ukraine }

Shot by Gestapo officer. Aged 50.

MARGARET MITCHELL
novelist
{ d. 11 August 1949, Atalanta GA, USA }

Drunk driver accident. Aged 48.

SYLVIA PLATH
poet
{ d. 11 February 1963, London, England }

Gassed in her own oven. Aged 30.

EDGAR ALLAN POE
poet, novelist
{ d. 7 October 1849, Baltimore MA, USA }

Found in the street semi-conscious and dressed in clothes that weren't his. Medical records have been lost. Aged 40.

HART CRANE
poet
{ d. 27 April 1932, Gulf of Florida, USA }

Drowned. Aged 32.

CHRISTOPHER MARLOWE
playwright
{ d. 30 May 1593, London, England }

Stabbed. Aged 29.

DAN ANDERSSON
poet, critic
{ d. 16 September 1920, Stockholm, Sweden }

Hydrogen cyanide poisoning from bedbug extermination procedure. Aged 32.

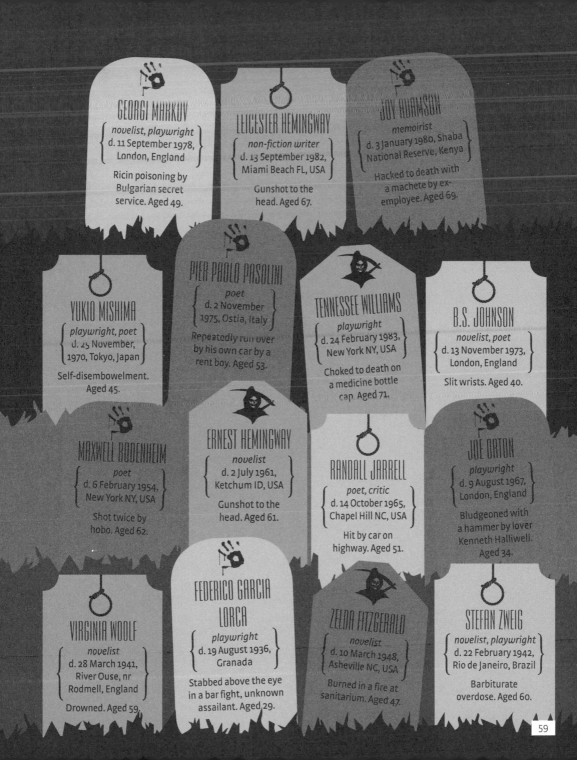

GEORGI MARKOV

novelist, playwright
d. 11 September 1978,
London, England

Ricin poisoning by
Bulgarian secret
service. Aged 49.

LEICESTER HEMINGWAY

non-fiction writer
d. 13 September 1982,
Miami Beach FL, USA

Gunshot to the
head. Aged 67.

JOY ADAMSON

memoirist
d. 3 January 1980, Shaba
National Reserve, Kenya

Hacked to death with
a machete by ex-
employee. Aged 69.

YUKIO MISHIMA

playwright, poet
d. 25 November,
1970, Tokyo, Japan

Self-disembowelment.
Aged 45.

PIER PAOLO PASOLINI

poet
d. 2 November
1975, Ostia, Italy

Repeatedly run over
by his own car by a
rent boy. Aged 53.

TENNESSEE WILLIAMS

playwright
d. 24 February 1983,
New York NY, USA

Choked to death on
a medicine bottle
cap. Aged 71.

B.S. JOHNSON

novelist, poet
d. 13 November 1973,
London, England

Slit wrists. Aged 40.

MAXWELL BODENHEIM

poet
d. 6 February 1954,
New York NY, USA

Shot twice by
hobo. Aged 62.

ERNEST HEMINGWAY

novelist
d. 2 July 1961,
Ketchum ID, USA

Gunshot to the
head. Aged 61.

RANDALL JARRELL

poet, critic
d. 14 October 1965,
Chapel Hill NC, USA

Hit by car on
highway. Aged 51.

JOE ORTON

playwright
d. 9 August 1967,
London, England

Bludgeoned with
a hammer by lover
Kenneth Halliwell.
Aged 34.

VIRGINIA WOOLF

novelist
d. 28 March 1941,
River Ouse, nr
Rodmell, England

Drowned. Aged 59.

**FEDERICO GARCIA
LORCA**

playwright
d. 19 August 1936,
Granada

Stabbed above the eye
in a bar fight, unknown
assailant. Aged 29.

ZELDA FITZGERALD

novelist
d. 10 March 1948,
Asheville NC, USA

Burned in a fire at
sanitarium. Aged 47.

STEFAN ZWEIG

novelist, playwright
d. 22 February 1942,
Rio de Janeiro, Brazil

Barbiturate
overdose. Aged 60.

REMEMBRANCE	23%
MADELEINES	15%
TIME	10%
ART	9%
SOCIAL CLIMBING	7%
MOTHER	7%
HOMOSEXUALITY	7%
WRITER'S BLOCK	6%
MEALS	6%
THEATRE	4%
TAILORS	3%
CONFLICT	2%
SLEEP	1%

WHAT WAS ON **MARCEL PROUST**'S MIND?

Marcel Proust (1871–1922) is most famous for writing the seven-volume In Search Of Lost Time, *and for its inspiration being a bite of a little French fancy, dipped in tea. Written over the course of the last 13 years of his life, Proust's masterwork is filled with detail of memory, reflections on perception, aspects of social interaction and contemporary French society. From it we can deduce that this is mostly what was on his mind.*

FELINE **FEELINGS**

Novelists love cats, as much for their capacity to embody
malevolence as for cuteness and faithfulness. Here is a literary
cat matrix with the famous felines of imagination plotted on it.

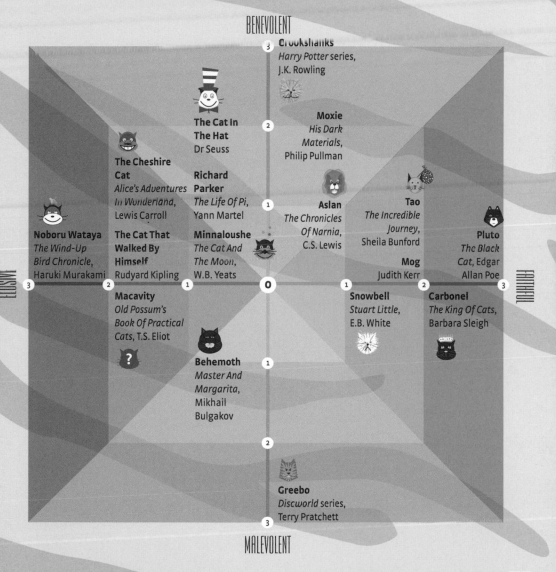

BENEVOLENT

3 **Crookshanks**
Harry Potter series,
J.K. Rowling

2 **Moxie**
*His Dark
Materials*,
Philip Pullman

**The Cat In
The Hat**
Dr Seuss

**The Cheshire
Cat**
*Alice's Adventures
In Wonderland*,
Lewis Carroll

**Richard
Parker**
The Life Of Pi,
Yann Martel

1 **Aslan**
*The Chronicles
Of Narnia*,
C.S. Lewis

Tao
*The Incredible
Journey*,
Sheila Bunford

Noboru Wataya
*The Wind-Up
Bird Chronicle*,
Haruki Murakami

**The Cat That
Walked By
Himself**
Rudyard Kipling

Minnaloushe
*The Cat And
The Moon*,
W.B. Yeats

Mog
Judith Kerr

Pluto
*The Black
Cat*, Edgar
Allan Poe

ELUSIVE 3   2   1   **0**   1   2   3 **FAITHFUL**

Macavity
*Old Possum's
Book Of Practical
Cats*, T.S. Eliot

Snowbell
Stuart Little,
E.B. White

Carbonel
The King Of Cats,
Barbara Sleigh

1 **Behemoth**
*Master And
Margarita*,
Mikhail
Bulgakov

2

Greebo
Discworld series,
Terry Pratchett

3

MALEVOLENT

LINES OF INFLUENCE:
SHAKESPEARE

Before Shakespeare there were poets and playwrights that he read and was inspired by. During his lifetime he worked with other playwrights, and read essayists and poets for inspiration. In the two centuries after his death, poets, playwrights, essayists and critics used his work, some of them earning the reputation as the 'Shakespeare' of their homeland. Tracing his lines of influence from 70 BC to the 19th century.

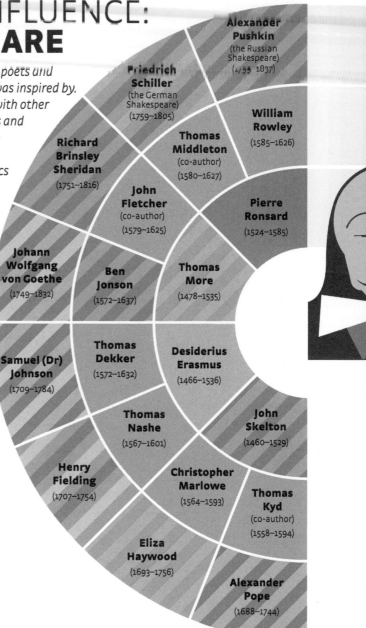

Alexander Pushkin (the Russian Shakespeare) (1799–1837)

Friedrich Schiller (the German Shakespeare) (1759–1805)

William Rowley (1585–1626)

Thomas Middleton (co-author) (1580–1627)

Richard Brinsley Sheridan (1751–1816)

John Fletcher (co-author) (1579–1625)

Pierre Ronsard (1524–1585)

Johann Wolfgang von Goethe (1749–1832)

Ben Jonson (1572–1637)

Thomas More (1478–1535)

Samuel (Dr) Johnson (1709–1784)

Thomas Dekker (1572–1632)

Desiderius Erasmus (1466–1536)

Thomas Nashe (1567–1601)

John Skelton (1460–1529)

Henry Fielding (1707–1754)

Christopher Marlowe (1564–1593)

Thomas Kyd (co-author) (1558–1594)

Eliza Haywood (1693–1756)

Alexander Pope (1688–1744)

OUTER WHEEL:

POST-SHAKESPEARE

MIDDLE WHEEL:

SHAKESPEARE CONTEMPORARY

INNER WHEEL:

PRE-SHAKESPEARE

John Milton
(1608–1674)

Andrew Marvell
(1621–1678)

Michel de Montaigne
(1533–1592)

Philip Sidney
(1554–1586)

Jean-Baptiste Molière
(the French Shakespeare)
(1622–1673)

Virgil
(70–19BC)

Francis Bacon
(1561–1626)

Dante Alighieri
(1266–1321)

Edmund Spenser
(1553–1599)

John Dryden
(1631–1700)

Geoffrey Chaucer
(1343–1400)

George Peele
(co-author)
(1553–1596)

Aphra Behn
(1640–1689)

John Lydgate
(1370–1451)

John Donne
(1572–1631)

John Florio
(the Italian Shakespeare)
(1553–1625)

Jonathan Swift
(1667–1745)

Miguel de Cervantes
(the Spanish Shakespeare)
(1547–1616)

William Congreve
(1670–1729)

John Gay
(1685–1732)

KEY:
- ■ POET
- ■ PLAYWRIGHT
- ■ ESSAYIST
- ■ NOVELIST
- ■ CRITIC

FUTURE **PAST**

Here are the novelists who have created fictional future worlds in which people interact with technology that was unknown at the time of writing. Some of the predictions can be traced to scientific work being done at the time – Jules Verne had seen sketches for a German submarine three years before writing about Nautilus, so it isn't included here – others are pure imagination. Until later.

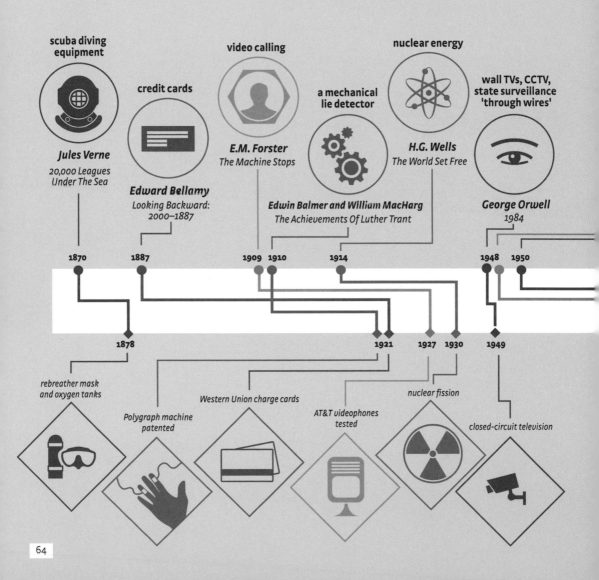

scuba diving equipment

credit cards

video calling

a mechanical lie detector

nuclear energy

wall TVs, CCTV, state surveillance 'through wires'

Jules Verne
20,000 Leagues Under The Sea

Edward Bellamy
Looking Backward: 2000–1887

E.M. Forster
The Machine Stops

Edwin Balmer and William MacHarg
The Achievements Of Luther Trant

H.G. Wells
The World Set Free

George Orwell
1984

1870   1887   1909 1910   1914   1948   1950

1878   1921   1927 1930   1949

rebreather mask and oxygen tanks

Polygraph machine patented

Western Union charge cards

AT&T videophones tested

nuclear fission

closed-circuit television

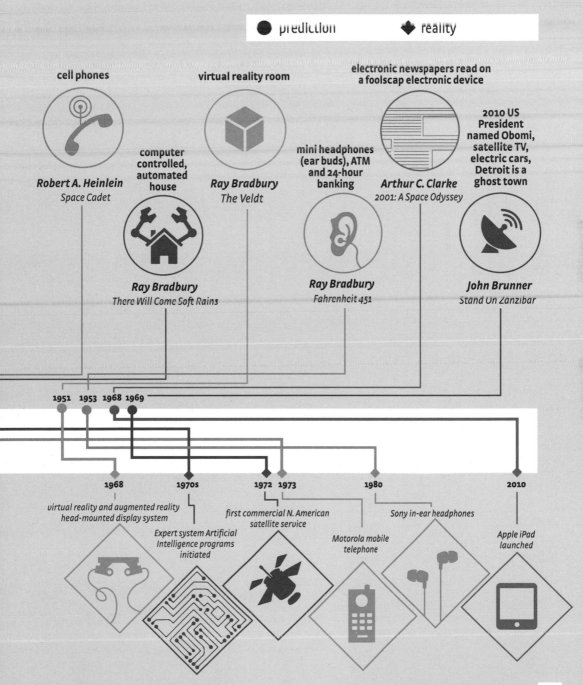

prediction ● reality ◆

cell phones

computer controlled, automated house

virtual reality room

mini headphones (ear buds), ATM and 24-hour banking

electronic newspapers read on a foolscap electronic device

2010 US President named Obomi, satellite TV, electric cars, Detroit is a ghost town

Robert A. Heinlein
Space Cadet

Ray Bradbury
The Veldt

Arthur C. Clarke
2001: A Space Odyssey

Ray Bradbury
There Will Come Soft Rains

Ray Bradbury
Fahrenheit 451

John Brunner
Stand On Zanzibar

1951 1953 1968 1969

1968
virtual reality and augmented reality head-mounted display system

1970s
Expert system Artificial Intelligence programs initiated

1972 1973
first commercial N. American satellite service

1980
Sony in-ear headphones

Motorola mobile telephone

2010
Apple iPad launched

65

LIVING
WRIT LARGE

Joseph Conrad (1857–1924)
The Nigger Of The Narcissus (1897), Heart Of Darkness (1899),
Lord Jim (1900), Typhoon (1902), The Shadow Line (1917).

Mark Twain (1835–1910)
The Adventures Of Tom Sawyer (1876),
The Adventures of Huckleberry Finn (1884)

Herman Melville (1819–1891)
Typee (1846), Omoo (1847), Mardi (1849), Moby Dick (1851)

Jack London (1876–1916)
The Call Of The Wild (1903), White Fang (1906)

George Orwell (1903–1950)
Burmese Days (1934)

Jack London (1876–1916)
The Sea-Wolf (1904)

P.C. Wren (1875–1941)
Beau Geste (1924)

Mark Twain (1835–1910)
Roughing It (1872)

Charles Dickens (1812–1870)
Hard Times (1854)

| steamboat pilot (1859–1861) | gold prospector (1897–1899) | merchant seaman (1890–1892) | silver miner (1862) | |

| merchant seaman (1874–1893) | merchant seaman (1839–1844) | policeman (1922–1926) | foreign legion soldier (1917–1922) | blacking factory hand (1824) |

'Write what you know' is a cliché of writing courses everywhere, and as these international best-selling authors prove, it's advice that works. All of the authors here translated their civilian work experiences into novels. Some lived more adventurous lives than others, but as Charles Bukowski showed, even working in a post office can be turned into great fiction.

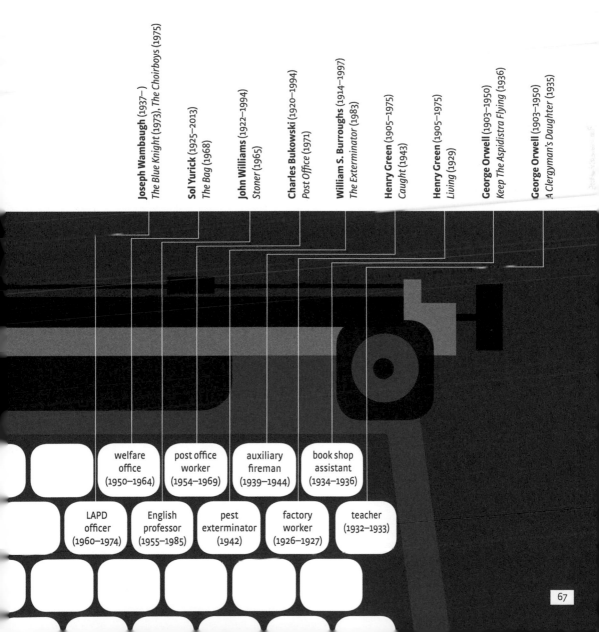

Joseph Wambaugh (1937–)
The Blue Knight (1973), *The Choirboys* (1975)

Sol Yurick (1925–2013)
The Bag (1968)

John Williams (1922–1994)
Stoner (1965)

Charles Bukowski (1920–1994)
Post Office (1971)

William S. Burroughs (1914–1997)
The Exterminator (1983)

Henry Green (1905–1975)
Caught (1943)

Henry Green (1905–1975)
Living (1929)

George Orwell (1903–1950)
Keep The Aspidistra Flying (1936)

George Orwell (1903–1950)
A Clergyman's Daughter (1935)

welfare office (1950–1964)

post office worker (1954–1969)

auxiliary fireman (1939–1944)

book shop assistant (1934–1936)

LAPD officer (1960–1974)

English professor (1955–1985)

pest exterminator (1942)

factory worker (1926–1927)

teacher (1932–1933)

FLOGGING A **DEAD HORSE**

Just because an author dies, it doesn't mean that their characters have to. As well as manuscripts finished but not published before death, there are always sequels, prequels and further adventures of, written in the style of the originals. These 15 famous originals have been extended well beyond the death of their originator.

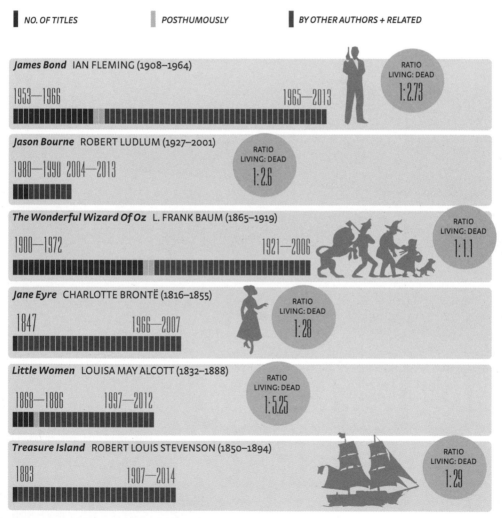

■ *NO. OF TITLES*　　■ *POSTHUMOUSLY*　　■ *BY OTHER AUTHORS + RELATED*

James Bond　IAN FLEMING (1908–1964)

1953–1966　　　　　　　　　　　　　1965–2013

RATIO LIVING: DEAD
1:2.73

Jason Bourne　ROBERT LUDLUM (1927–2001)

1980–1990　2004–2013

RATIO LIVING: DEAD
1:2.6

The Wonderful Wizard Of Oz　L. FRANK BAUM (1865–1919)

1900–1972　　　　　　　　　　　1921–2006

RATIO LIVING: DEAD
1:1.1

Jane Eyre　CHARLOTTE BRONTË (1816–1855)

1847　　　　　　1966–2007

RATIO LIVING: DEAD
1:28

Little Women　LOUISA MAY ALCOTT (1832–1888)

1868–1886　　1997–2012

RATIO LIVING: DEAD
1:5.25

Treasure Island　ROBERT LOUIS STEVENSON (1850–1894)

1883　　　　　1907–2014

RATIO LIVING: DEAD
1:29

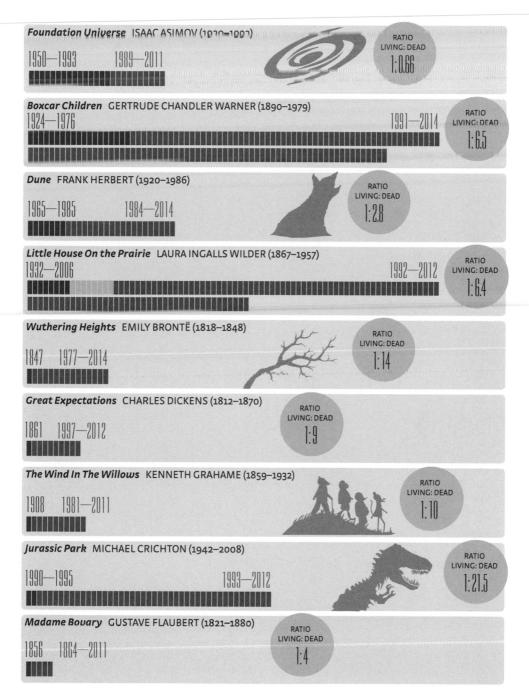

Foundation Universe ISAAC ASIMOV (1920–1992)

1950—1993   1989—2011

RATIO
LIVING: DEAD
1:0.66

Boxcar Children GERTRUDE CHANDLER WARNER (1890–1979)

1924—1976   1991—2014

RATIO
LIVING: DEAD
1:6.5

Dune FRANK HERBERT (1920–1986)

1965—1985   1984—2014

RATIO
LIVING: DEAD
1:2.8

Little House On the Prairie LAURA INGALLS WILDER (1867–1957)

1932—2006   1992—2012

RATIO
LIVING: DEAD
1:6.4

Wuthering Heights EMILY BRONTË (1818–1848)

1847   1977—2014

RATIO
LIVING: DEAD
1:14

Great Expectations CHARLES DICKENS (1812–1870)

1861   1997—2012

RATIO
LIVING: DEAD
1:9

The Wind In The Willows KENNETH GRAHAME (1859–1932)

1908   1981—2011

RATIO
LIVING: DEAD
1:10

Jurassic Park MICHAEL CRICHTON (1942–2008)

1990—1995   1993—2012

RATIO
LIVING: DEAD
1:21.5

Madame Bovary GUSTAVE FLAUBERT (1821–1880)

1856   1864—2011

RATIO
LIVING: DEAD
1:4

Lewis Carroll	*Alice's Adventures In Wonderland*	1865
Lewis Carroll	*Through The Looking Glass*	1871
L. Frank Baum	*The Wonderful Wizard Of Oz*	1900
J.M. Barrie	*Peter Pan*	1911
Frances Hodgson Burnett	*The Secret Garden*	1911
C.S. Lewis	*The Lion, The Witch And The Wardrobe*	1950
Philippa Pearce	*Tom's Midnight Garden*	1958
Norton Juster	*The Phantom Tollbooth*	1961
Pierre Berton	*The Secret World Of Og*	1961
Madeleine L'Engle	*A Wrinkle In Time*	1962
Maurice Sendak	*Where The Wild Things Are*	1963
Clive King	*Stig Of The Dump*	1963
Roald Dahl	*Charlie And The Chocolate Factory*	1964
Michael Ende	*The Neverending Story*	1983
Eva Ibbotson	*The Secret Of Platform 13*	1994
Enid Blyton	*Faraway Tree series*	1939–1951
David McKee	*Mr Benn series*	1967–
Philip Pullman	*His Dark Materials trilogy*	1995–2000
J.K. Rowling	*Harry Potter series*	1997–2007
Cornelia Funke	*Inkheart trilogy*	2003–2007

PORTAL TO **ANOTHER WORLD**

Good books offer the reader a window on to another world, and good children's books transport their reader (or listener) into different worlds. Especially those in which a seemingly ordinary object turns out to be a doorway to a parallel universe for the characters in the story. These are the 20 most famous portals in children's literature.

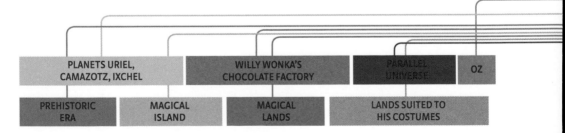

PLANETS URIEL, CAMAZOTZ, IXCHEL

WILLY WONKA'S CHOCOLATE FACTORY

PARALLEL UNIVERSE

OZ

PREHISTORIC ERA

MAGICAL ISLAND

MAGICAL LANDS

LANDS SUITED TO HIS COSTUMES

Alice
Alice
Dorothy and Toto
Wendy, John, Michael
Mary
Lucy, Peter, Susan, Edmund
Tom
Milo
Penny, Pamela, Patsy, Peter
Meg
Max
Barney
Charlie
Bastian
Hans, Gurkintrude, Cor, Odge
Jo, Bessie, Fanny
Mr Benn
Lyra, Will
Harry, Ron, Hermione
Meggie

rabbit hole
mirror
twister
window
key
wardrobe
back door and clock striking 13
toy car and tollbooth
trapdoor
tesseract (a fold in time)
boat
chalk pit
chocolate bar
book
railway platform 13, King's Cross
tall tree
changing room
subtle knife
railway platform 9 3/4, King's Cross
father talking

ISLAND OF WILD BEASTS
WONDERLAND
NEVERLAND
OG
FANTASTICA
HOGWARTS SCHOOL

SECRET GARDEN
KINGDOM OF WISDOM
VICTORIAN GARDEN
INKWORLD
NARNIA

DEGREES OF GOTHIC

Gothic literature has its beginnings in the late 18th century with Horace Walpole and Ann Radcliffe. They set a template that has been followed and improved upon by numerous writers ever since. Here are the 13 key ingredients of any true Gothic novel, and the great works of the genre gauged by how many each contains.

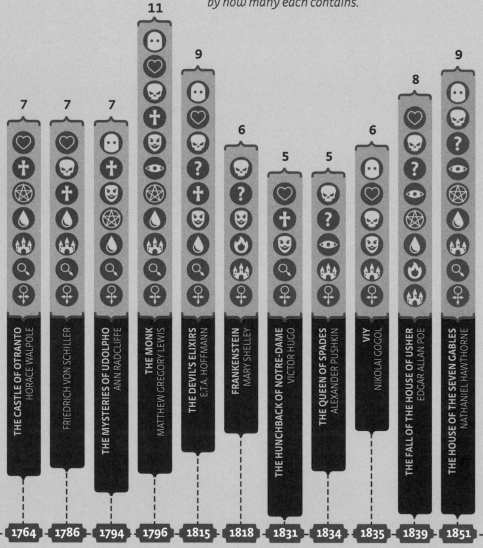

11 THE MONK — MATTHEW GREGORY LEWIS — 1796

9 THE DEVIL'S ELIXIRS — E.T.A. HOFFMANN — 1815

9 THE HOUSE OF THE SEVEN GABLES — NATHANIEL HAWTHORNE — 1851

8 THE FALL OF THE HOUSE OF USHER — EDGAR ALLAN POE — 1839

7 THE CASTLE OF OTRANTO — HORACE WALPOLE — 1764

7 FRIEDRICH VON SCHILLER — 1786

7 THE MYSTERIES OF UDOLPHO — ANN RADCLIFFE — 1794

6 FRANKENSTEIN — MARY SHELLEY — 1818

6 VIY — NIKOLAI GOGOL — 1835

5 THE HUNCHBACK OF NOTRE-DAME — VICTOR HUGO — 1831

5 THE QUEEN OF SPADES — ALEXANDER PUSHKIN — 1834

Timeline: 1764 – 1786 – 1794 – 1796 – 1815 – 1818 – 1831 – 1834 – 1835 – 1839 – 1851

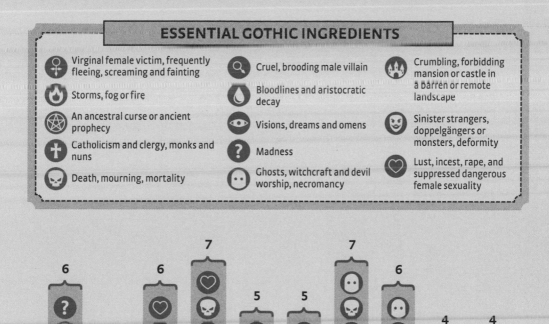

ESSENTIAL GOTHIC INGREDIENTS

- Virginal female victim, frequently fleeing, screaming and fainting
- Storms, fog or fire
- An ancestral curse or ancient prophecy
- Catholicism and clergy, monks and nuns
- Death, mourning, mortality
- Cruel, brooding male villain
- Bloodlines and aristocratic decay
- Visions, dreams and omens
- Madness
- Ghosts, witchcraft and devil worship, necromancy
- Crumbling, forbidding mansion or castle in a barren or remote landscape
- Sinister strangers, doppelgängers or monsters, deformity
- Lust, incest, rape, and suppressed dangerous female sexuality

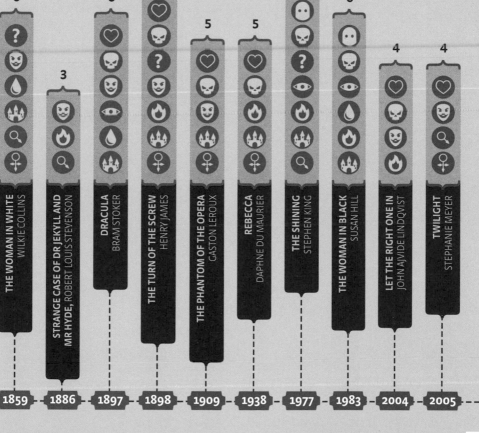

| 6 | 3 | 6 | 7 | 5 | 5 | 7 | 6 | 4 | 4 |

THE WOMAN IN WHITE — WILKIE COLLINS

STRANGE CASE OF DR JEKYLL AND MR HYDE, ROBERT LOUIS STEVENSON

DRACULA — BRAM STOKER

THE TURN OF THE SCREW — HENRY JAMES

THE PHANTOM OF THE OPERA — GASTON LEROUX

REBECCA — DAPHNE DU MAURIER

THE SHINING — STEPHEN KING

THE WOMAN IN BLACK — SUSAN HILL

LET THE RIGHT ONE IN — JOHN AJVIDE LINDQVIST

TWILIGHT — STEPHANIE MEYER

| 1859 | 1886 | 1897 | 1898 | 1909 | 1938 | 1977 | 1983 | 2004 | 2005 |

HERE BE **MONSTERS**

The Greeks knew how to create a good monster. Their fantastical creatures have stayed in the human psyche for centuries due partly to the retelling of original myths, and also because novelists and poets drew inspiration and rewrote them. Here are the most memorable interpretations of Greek monsters.

ENCELADUS
Giant with serpent-like limbs

HYPERION
John Keats
1819
Referenced

PIERRE
Herman Melville
1852
Appears in a dream

THE LOST HERO
Rick Riordan
2010
Primary villain

CENTAUR
Head and torso of a man, body of a horse

THE CHRONICLES OF NARNIA
C.S. Lewis
1950–1956
Creatures with reason

HARRY POTTER
J.K. Rowling
1997–2007
Centaurs live in the forbidden forest

THE CENTAUR
John Updike
1963
Reason and nature clash in a rural town

HARPIES
Bird women

HIS DARK MATERIALS
Philip Pullman
1995
Includes a race of winged women

THE LAST UNICORN
Peter S. Beagle
1968
The character Celeano embodies a harpy

A SONG OF ICE AND FIRE
George R.R. Martin
1996
Symbol of slaver families

BRIAREUS
1 of 3 giants with 100 hands and 50 heads

INFERNO
Dante
1308–1321
A giant in the 9th circle of hell

DON QUIXOTE
Miguel de Cervantes
1605
Believes windmills to be briareus

PARADISE LOST
John Milton
1667
Compared to fallen Satan

MANTICORE
Human head, sharp teeth, lion's body, scorpion's tail

THE MANTICORE
Robertson Davies
1972
Elements of subconscious manifest as manticore

HARRY POTTER
J.K. Rowling
1997–2007
Hagrid owns a manticore

MANY WATERS
Madeleine L'Engle
1986
Animal who eats other animals

MEDUSA

Gorgon, female monster with snakes for hair

THE LIGHTNING THIEF
Rick Riordan
2005
Main antagonist

A TALE OF TWO CITIES
Charles Dickens
1859
French aristocracy compared to Gorgons

MACBETH
William Shakespeare
1606
The three witches

ANTAEUS

A half-giant

INFERNO
Dante
1308–1321
Depicted as half-frozen giant

ANTAEUS (POEM)
Seamus Heaney
1975
Retelling

ANTAEUS (SHORT STORY)
Borden Deal
1962
Retelling

FAHRENHEIT 451
Ray Bradbury
1953
Metaphor for over-indulgence

LAMIA

Beautiful, evil queen

LAMIA
John Keats
1820
Tells of Hermes finding a lamia trapped in the body of a serpent

AURORA LEIGH
Elizabeth Barrett Browning
1856
Dead mother appears as lamia

ELEMENTALS: STORIES OF FIRE AND ICE
A.S. Byatt
1998
Lamia begins to be made human

NEVERWHERE
Neil Gaiman
1996
Lamia as warmth-drinking vampire

MINOTAUR

Head of a bull, body of a man

THE LION, THE WITCH AND THE WARDROBE
C.S. Lewis
1950
Followers of the Queen

THE HOUSE OF ASTERION
Jorge Borges
1947
Retelling the story of the minotaur

HOUSE OF LEAVES
Mark Z. Danielewski
2000
Minotaur and labyrinth central

STRANGE CASE OF DR JEKYLL AND MR HYDE
Robert Louis Stevenson
1886
Half man, half beast

PAN

Half man, half goat

ENDYMION
John Keats
1818
Festival of Pan

THE WIND IN THE WILLOWS
Kenneth Grahame
1908
Pan helps Rat and Mole

THE GREAT GOD PAN
Arthur Machen
1890
Symbol for power of nature

THE BLESSING OF PAN
Lord Dunsany
1927
Has a revival of worship of Pan

JITTERBUG PERFUME
Tom Robbins
1984
Pan appears throughout

IT'S THE END OF THE WORLD **(AGAIN)**

The fashion for writing and reading dystopian novels of the
20th century peaked with Cold War hysteria, but showed signs
of a revival in interest just after the turn of this century.

We Yevgeny Zamyatin (1921)

Brave New World Aldous Huxley (1932)

It Can't Happen Here Sinclair Lewis (1935)

Out Of The Silent Planet C.S. Lewis (1938)

Darkness At Noon Arthur Koestler (1940)

1984 George Orwell (1948)

The Day Of The Triffids John Wyndham (1951)

Fahrenheit 451 Ray Bradbury (1953)

The City And The Stars Arthur C. Clarke (1956)

Atlas Shrugged Ayn Rand (1957)

A Clockwork Orange Anthony Burgess (1962)

Logan's Run William F. Nolan, George Clayton Johnson (1967)

1920s

1930s

1940s

1950s

1960s

This Perfect Day Ira Levin (1970)

High Rise J.G. Ballard (1975)

Riddley Walker Russell Hoban (1980)

V For Vendetta Alan Moore, David Lloyd (1988–89)

Virtual Light William Gibson (1993)

Noughts And Crosses Malorie Blackman (2001)

Oryx And Crake Margaret Atwood (2003)

The Road Cormac McCarthy (2006)

The Hunger Games Suzanne Collins (2008)

Rondo John Maher (2010)

1970s

1980s

1990s

2000s

2010s

77

UNESCO'S **MOST TRANSLATED**

The United Nations Organization for Education, Science and Culture compiled the top 30 authors by total of works each had in translation around the world, between 1979 and 2017. Here they are, with the number of each of the authors' original published works (short stories are collections) by genre.

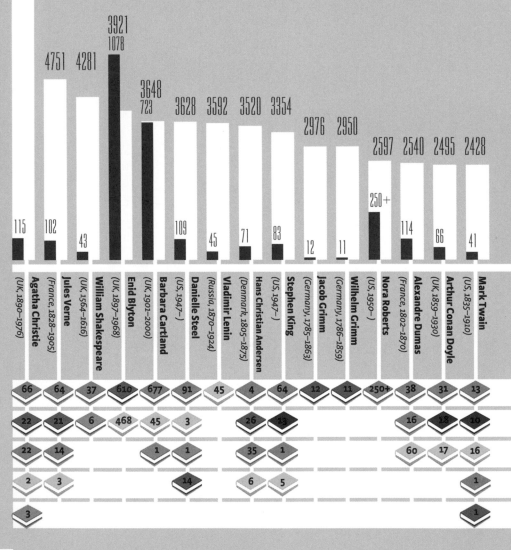

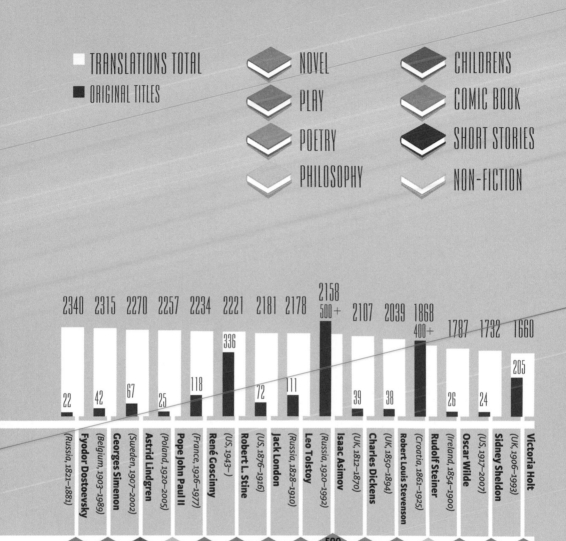

LES MISERABLES
VICTOR HUGO
1862

0.18% *of work* — 823 *words*

SODOM AND GOMORRAH
VOLUME 4
of
In Search Of Lost Time
MARCEL PROUST
1913

0.45% *of work* — 944 *words*

ABSOLOM, ABSOLOM!
WILLIAM FAULKNER
1936

1.12% *of work* — 1,288 *words*

THE ROTTER'S CLUB
JONATHAN COE
2001

7.9% *of work* — 13,955 *words*

PERSONAL DAYS
ED PARKS
2008

18.8% *of work* — 16,000 *words*

DANCING LESSONS FOR THE ADVANCED IN AGE
BOHUMIL HRABAL
1964

100% *of work* — 20,000 *words*

THE LONGEST **SENTENCE**

Take a deep breath, and then begin reading. The longest sentence published in a single volume is currently 180,000 words long, and constitutes the whole of the book, in its original French language. Victor Hugo began the bizarre trend in the 19th century, since when these works have expanded on his idea of using the full stop sparingly.

THE ASSIGNMENT

FRIEDRICH DÜRRENMATT

1986

4.1% of work   1,600 words

ULYSSES

JAMES JOYCE

1922

1.7% of work   4,391 words

AUTUMN OF THE PATRIARCH

GABRIEL GARCÍA MÁRQUEZ

1975

14.6% of work   13,650 words

GATES OF PARADISE

JERZY ANDRZEJEWSKI

1960

99.98% of work   40,000 words

RAY OF THE STAR

LAIRD HUNT

2009

100% of work   58,000 words

ZONE

MATHIAS ÉNARD

2008

100% of work   180,000 words

= percentage of work

= 1,000 words

Brother William of Baskerville
A Sherlock Holmes-style detective monk

Adso of Melk
William's much younger assistant (see Dr Watson)

THE LIBRARY/LABYRINTH

William and Adso use wool to find their way in and out of rooms looking for clues.

One room has hallucinogenic gas.

The centre of the library holds the secret to the Name Of The Rose.

Ubertino   Michael   Bernardo   Bertrand

Rabano

Patrick

Abo of Fossanova – The abbot of the Benedictine monastery. Together with the librarian, his assistant and Jorge da Burgos, he is the only one who knows about the secrets of the library.

Jorge da Burgos – An old, blind former librarian of the monastery. A caricature of writer Jorge Luis Borges.

Severinus of Sankt Wendel – Herbalist who helps William.

Malachi of Hildesheim – Librarian.

Berengar of Arundel – Assistant librarian.

Adelmo of Otranto – Illuminator, novice. The first murder victim.

Venantius of Salvemec – Translator of manuscripts from Greek and Arabic and devoted to Aristotle.

Benno of Uppsala – Scandinavian student of rhetoric.

Alinardo of Grottaferrata – Eldest monk. Everyone believes he suffers from senile dementia but he will play a fundamental role in solving the mystery.

Remigio of Varagine – Cellarer. Name derived from Dominican friar Jacobus de Voragine, author of a Latin collection of the lives of the Saints.

Salvatore of Montferrat – Monk, associate of Remigio. Speaks a mixture of Latin and lewd vernacular Italian.

Nicholas of Morimondo – Glazier.

Aymaro of Alessandria – Italian transcriber. Gossipy and sneering.

Waldo of Hereford, Patrick of Clonmacnois, Rabano of Toledo – Transcribers.

Ubertino of Casale – Franciscan friar in exile, friend of William.

Michael of Cesena – Leader of Spiritual Franciscans.

Bernardo Gui – Inquisitor from the Dominican order.

Bertrand del Poggetto – Cardinal and leader of the Papal legation.

Peasant girl from the village below the monastery – Adso has sex with her in the kitchen.

WHAT IS THE NAME OF THE ROSE?

Italian author Umberto Eco's brilliant detective thriller, set in a 13th-century monastery, is told with the intrigue of a 19th-century yarn. The action focuses on the labyrinthine library, shown here with the levels of access allowed to the story's characters.

Benno

Alinardo

Abo

Severinus

Remigio

Nicholas

Adso of Melk   Jorge da Burgos

William of Baskerville

Malachi

Berengar

Salvatore

Venantius

Waldo

Aymaro

Adelmo

MURDERS

1. **Adelmo** – Dies in a storm. There are rumours in the monastery that his death may be a sign of the arrival of the Antichrist.

2. **Venantiuso** – Found drowned in a washbowl full of the blood of pigs.

3. **Berengaro** – Drowned in a bath in the *balnea*.

4. **Severinuso** – Head smashed with a copper armillary sphere.

5. **Malachi** – Dies in front of the friars at morning prayers.

All of the corpses have black stains on their tongue and fingers.

JUDGING A BOOK **BY ITS COVER**

With the majority of books sold online rather than in-store, the tiny, cell phone-sized front cover image has to be able to convey content at a glance. Which is why the majority of genre-leading best-sellers tend to look the same, with only the author's name immediately recognizable. Here are the style rules for the eight best-selling genres.

Silver or gold foil title larger than author, blood red, deep purple or midnight-blue colours, male or female face-on to cover, partly dressed

Light, pastel colours, flowers real or drawn, female legs, hands, arms, no face

GENRE

- Best-selling blockbuster mystery
- Classic literature
- Historical fiction
- Romantic suspense
- Erotica
- Vampire
- Chick-lit
- Teen horror

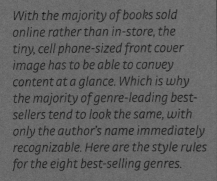

Dark grey or black with semi-naked male or couple, no faces shown

A section of a painting of a woman from the era of the novel's setting, script font title

Old-fashioned artwork, in style of original era of publication

Author's name in silver or gold foil on the top 2/3rds of the page, the title on the lower 3rd, background a 'painted' landscape

Author name on the top 2/3rds of image, title bottom 3rd, background one-colour indeterminate photo image, possibly with a figure in long-shot

Monochrome photo of girl, dressed in Victorian or early 20th-century clothes, or of angel/graveyard, 'shaky' handwritten font

DEATH BY **SHAKESPEARE**

William Shakespeare's tragedies are renowned for the number of deaths depicted (although often acted off-stage), his history and 'problem' plays have a few characters meeting their maker, too. Here's how many and in which plays.

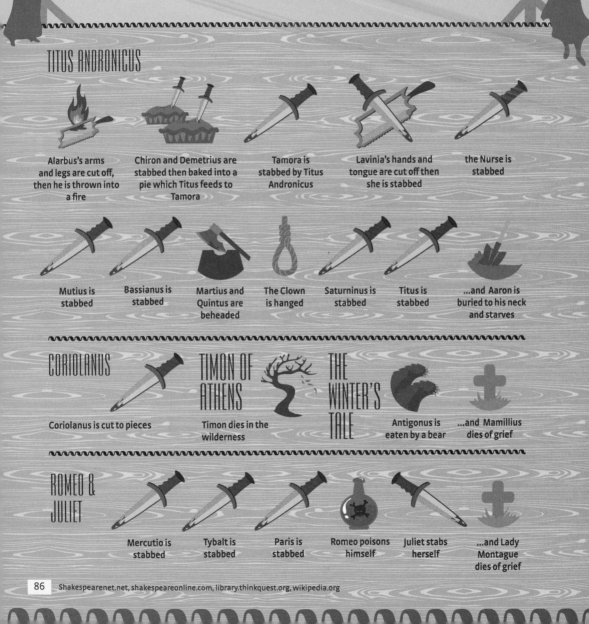

TITUS ANDRONICUS

Alarbus's arms and legs are cut off, then he is thrown into a fire

Chiron and Demetrius are stabbed then baked into a pie which Titus feeds to Tamora

Tamora is stabbed by Titus Andronicus

Lavinia's hands and tongue are cut off then she is stabbed

the Nurse is stabbed

Mutius is stabbed

Bassianus is stabbed

Martius and Quintus are beheaded

The Clown is hanged

Saturninus is stabbed

Titus is stabbed

...and Aaron is buried to his neck and starves

CORIOLANUS

Coriolanus is cut to pieces

TIMON OF ATHENS

Timon dies in the wilderness

THE WINTER'S TALE

Antigonus is eaten by a bear

...and Mamillius dies of grief

ROMEO & JULIET

Mercutio is stabbed

Tybalt is stabbed

Paris is stabbed

Romeo poisons himself

Juliet stabs herself

...and Lady Montague dies of grief

Shakespearenet.net, shakespeareonline.com, library.thinkquest.org, wikipedia.org

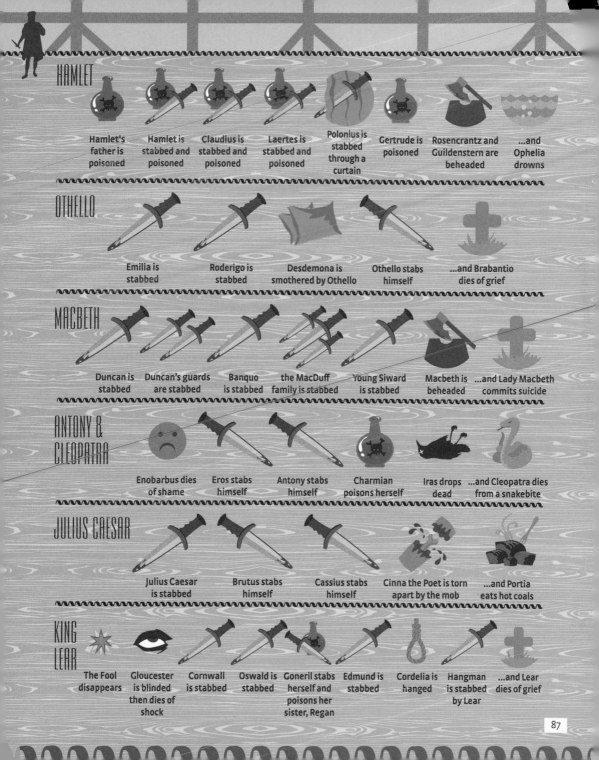

HAMLET

| Hamlet's father is poisoned | Hamlet is stabbed and poisoned | Claudius is stabbed and poisoned | Laertes is stabbed and poisoned | Polonius is stabbed through a curtain | Gertrude is poisoned | Rosencrantz and Guildenstern are beheaded | ...and Ophelia drowns |

OTHELLO

| Emilia is stabbed | Roderigo is stabbed | Desdemona is smothered by Othello | Othello stabs himself | ...and Brabantio dies of grief |

MACBETH

| Duncan is stabbed | Duncan's guards are stabbed | Banquo is stabbed | the MacDuff family is stabbed | Young Siward is stabbed | Macbeth is beheaded | ...and Lady Macbeth commits suicide |

ANTONY & CLEOPATRA

| Enobarbus dies of shame | Eros stabs himself | Antony stabs himself | Charmian poisons herself | Iras drops dead | ...and Cleopatra dies from a snakebite |

JULIUS CAESAR

| Julius Caesar is stabbed | Brutus stabs himself | Cassius stabs himself | Cinna the Poet is torn apart by the mob | ...and Portia eats hot coals |

KING LEAR

| The Fool disappears | Gloucester is blinded then dies of shock | Cornwall is stabbed | Oswald is stabbed | Goneril stabs herself and poisons her sister, Regan | Edmund is stabbed | Cordelia is hanged | Hangman is stabbed by Lear | ...and Lear dies of grief |

FROM STONE TABLET TO
DIGITAL TABLET

From scratches on a wall to scratches in the air, the history of man's published works has come a long way to nothing at all in the past 5,000 years.

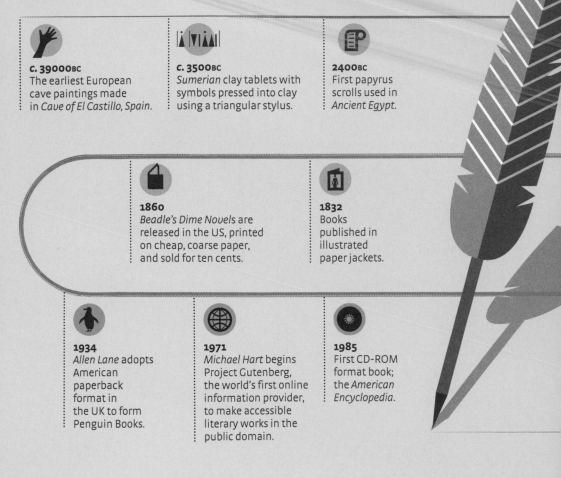

C. 39000BC
The earliest European cave paintings made in *Cave of El Castillo, Spain.*

C. 3500BC
Sumerian clay tablets with symbols pressed into clay using a triangular stylus.

2400BC
First papyrus scrolls used in *Ancient Egypt.*

1860
*Beadle's Dime Novel*s are released in the US, printed on cheap, coarse paper, and sold for ten cents.

1832
Books published in illustrated paper jackets.

1934
Allen Lane adopts American paperback format in the UK to form Penguin Books.

1971
Michael Hart begins Project Gutenberg, the world's first online information provider, to make accessible literary works in the public domain.

1985
First CD-ROM format book; the *American Encyclopedia*.

200BC
Wax tablet codex,
the beginning
of bound books used by
Greeks and *Romans*.

AD400–600
Illustrated, handwritten works in *Europe*
and the *Middle East* written on vellum-like
parchments made from calf, sheep,
or goat skins.

AD105
Paper invented by *Cai Lun*,
a Chinese eunuch, combining
'bark, hemp, old rags,
and used fish nets'.

AD1041
The Chinese invent movable
type; unsuccessful due
to the complexity
of Chinese alphabet.

1774
Chlorine is discovered,
later used to bleach
paper for print.

1501
Aldo Manuzio
designs and
produces the first
octavo book.

AD1440
Johannes Gutenberg completes
the first printing press, and
prints the 42-line *Gutenberg
Bible* in 1455.

1991
HTML code developed,
the internet made
available for commercial use.

1995
Jeff Bezos' Amazon.com
goes live, selling
books online.

1996
XML markup language
developed, streamlining
book production.

2011–2012
EPUB3 and HTML5
enable greater integration
of multimedia elements
within e-books.

2010
First *Apple iPad*
released
(plus iBooks
and iBooks Store).

2007
First *Amazon
Kindle* released,
as is EPUB
format.

2001–2006
e-books
developed for
the commercial
market.

GUESS THE
BEARDED WRITER

*From the 16th century to the present day,
authors have grown their facial hair and
trimmed it in interesting beard ways. Can you
guess which facial hair belongs to whom?
Clue: does not include George Eliot.*

FRENCH

FRENCH

1580–1590

1830–1840

AMERICAN

FRENCH

RUSSIAN

1840–1850

1850–1860

1865–1875

AMERICAN

SWEDISH

1870–1880

1880–1890

NATIONALITY

decade of key work

NORWEGIAN
1880–1890

ENGLISH
1894–1904

FRENCH
1910–1920

AMERICAN
1925–1935

GERMAN
1955–1965

TRINIDADIAN
1960–1970

CANADIAN
1970–1980

NORWEGIAN
2000–2010

TWO TRIBES: **THE MAHABHARATA**

The ancient Hindu text of the Mahabharata contains the eternal story of two warring tribal families who battle it out for supremacy and world domination. Each tribe member is either born with or attains a kind of super power.

KRISHNA
Incarnation of the God Vishnu. Wise, great tactician, advisor to the Pandavas and their protector. Imparts secret information on how to kill foes and ensures the Pandava victory.

PANDU
The father of the Pandavas, born pale, chose death over celibacy and founded a dynasty.

Pandavas
The Good Guys (the winners, with the gods on their side).

KUNTI
Wife of Pandu also bore children for the Sun God, the Wind God, the God of Judgement and the King of the Heavens. Raises her heroes' sons single-handedly.

YUDHISTHIRA
Son of the God of Judgement. Rightful heir to the throne. Emperor of the World. Unblemished by sin or untruth.

BHIMA
Son of the God of Wind. Strength of 1,000 elephants. Bully. Killer of the 100 Kaurava brothers. Huge appetite.

DRAUPADI
Wife to the five brothers. Queen of unsurpassed beauty. Protected by Krishna. Highly virtuous, intelligent and compassionate.

ARJUNA
Son of Indra, the Lord of Heaven. Main hero, an unbeatable archer, peerless warrior and invincible in water bodies. Possesses divine weaponry. Single-handedly slayed 200,000 warriors to avenge the murder of his son.

NAKULA and SAHADEVA
Very handsome sons of the Twin Gods of Sunset and Sunrise. Nakula is a superior horse handler, swordsman and a master at Ayurveda. Sahadeva is a great astrologer with knowledge of the future, cursed with death if he reveals it.

BHISHMA
Grand-uncle of Dhritarashtra and Pandu and great man. Son of the Goddess of the Ganges river. Vowed to serve. Chose time of his own death. Skilled in political science, attempted to minimize costs of the war.

SHAKUNI
Brother-in-law to Dhritarashtra, and resentful of him. Aims to destroy his clan. Possesses magic dice. Ruthless plotter, without honour.

पाण्डव
Kauravas
The Bad Guys (without the gods on their side).

DHRITARASHTRA
Blind king. Bore 100 sons. Ambitious, resentful of his brother's sons. Crusher of an iron statue.

DURYODHANA
Firstborn son. Hatred of Pandavas. Also Emperor of the World. Great military tactician. Acquires impenetrable body of diamond (except for lap). Symbolizes unfairness, deceit and lust.

GANDHARI
Wife to Dhritashtra. Self-imposed blindness. Bestows upon son impervious diamond-like body.

KARNA
Son of Sun God, firstborn of Kunti before marriage. Right hand to Duryodhana. Exemplary archer, possessed of divine weapon, denied opportunity because of low birth.

DUSHASANA
Second son. Obedient to older brother. Tried to disrobe Draupadi. Torn apart by Bhima, who drank his blood while Draupadi bathed her hair in it.

DRONACHARYA
Master archer, teacher of Arjuna. Bound by duty against love to fight with the Kauravas. Invincible warrior, slayed a vast amount of Pandava army. Committed suicide on being falsely informed of the death of his son.

HUSBAND - WIFE
PARENTS - SONS
RELATIVES
PROTECTORS/TRAINERS

93

$ 677M

Forrest Gump (1994)
Winston Groom (1986)

$ 441M

The Exorcist (1973)
William Peter Blatty (1971)

$ 424M

Dances With Wolves (1990)
Michael Blake (1988)

$ 263M

Jumanji (1995)
Chris Van Allsburg (1981)

$ 182M

Cape Fear (1991)
The Executioners
John D. MacDonald (1957)

$ 125M

First Blood (1982)
David Morrell (1972)

$ 111M

Cool Hand Luke (1967)
Donn Pearce (1965)

$ 66M

Scarface (1983)
Armitage Trail (1929)

$ 60M

Psycho (1960)
Robert Bloch (1959)

$ 48M

A Walk To Remember (2002)
Nicholas Sparks (1999)

$ 45M

A Clockwork Orange (1972)
Anthony Burgess (1962)

$ 38M

James And The
Giant Peach (1996)
Roald Dahl (1961)

$ 31M

The Bridge On The
River Kwai (1957)
Le Pont De La Rivière Kwai
Pierre Boulle (1952)

$ 14M

Vertigo (1958)
D'entre Les Morts Pierre Boileau
and Pierre Ayraud (1954)

$ 14M

To Catch A Thief (1955)
David F. Dodge (1952)

SUCCESSFUL ADAPTATIONS

ADAPTATION

Sometimes all a novel needs to become a best-seller is for a movie to be made of it. Smart authors write the screenplay of their novels — although not always — and re-publish the book of the film. Not that movie adaptations always work, and there have been many flop films of hit books.

Flim Title (Year)
Book Title *if different
Author (Year)

UNSUCCESSFUL ADAPTATIONS

$ 17K

As I Lay Dying (2013)
William Faulkner (1930)

$ 120K

The Trial (1962)
Franz Kafka (1925)

$ 223K

Swann In Love (1984)
In Search of Lost Time
Marcel Proust (1913)

$ 1M

Don Quixote (1992)
Miguel de Cervantes
(1605–1615)

$ 2M

Crash (1996)
J.G. Ballard (1973)

$ 2.3M

Ulysses (1967)
James Joyce (1922)

$ 3M

Mrs Dalloway (1997)
Virginia Woolf (1925)

$ 3M

Les Liaisons Dangereuses (1959)
Pierre Choderlos de Laclos (1782)

$ 4M

Myra Breckinridge (1970)
Gore Vidal (1969)

$ 4M

Tristram Shandy:
A Cock And Bull Story (2006)
(The Life And Opinions of
Tristram Shandy, Gentleman)
Laurence Sterne (1759)

$ 4M

The Naked Lunch (1991)
William S. Burroughs (1959)

$ 5M

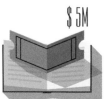

The Handmaid's Tale (1990)
Margaret Atwood (1985)

wikipedia.org, boxofficemojo.com

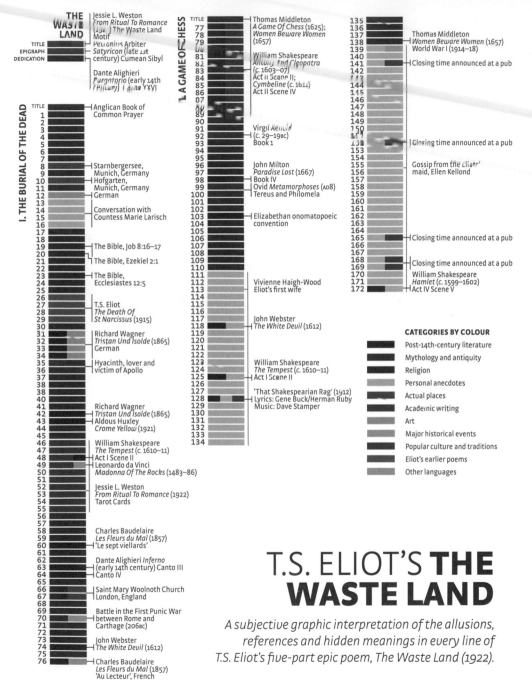

THE WASTE LAND

Jessie L. Weston *From Ritual To Romance* (1920) The Waste Land Motif

TITLE
EPIGRAPH
DEDICATION — Petronius Arbiter *Satyricon* (late 1st century) Cumean Sibyl

Dante Alighieri *Purgatorio* (early 14th century) Canto XXVI

I. THE BURIAL OF THE DEAD

TITLE
1
2
3
4
5
6
7 — Anglican Book of Common Prayer
8 — Starnbergersee, Munich, Germany
9
10 — Hofgarten, Munich, Germany
11
12 — German
13
14
15 — Conversation with Countess Marie Larisch
16
17
18
19 — The Bible, Job 8:16–17
20
21 — The Bible, Ezekiel 2:1
22
23
24 — The Bible, Ecclesiastes 12:5
25
26
27
28 — T.S. Eliot *The Death Of St Narcissus* (1915)
29
30
31
32 — Richard Wagner *Tristan Und Isolde* (1865)
33 — German
34
35
36 — Hyacinth, lover and victim of Apollo
37
38
39
40
41
42 — Richard Wagner *Tristan Und Isolde* (1865)
43
44 — Aldous Huxley *Crome Yellow* (1921)
45
46
47 — William Shakespeare *The Tempest* (c. 1610–11)
48 — Act I Scene II
49
50 — Leonardo da Vinci *Madonna Of The Rocks* (1483–86)
51
52
53
54 — Jessie L. Weston *From Ritual To Romance* (1922) Tarot Cards
55
56
57
58
59 — Charles Baudelaire *Les Fleurs du Mal* (1857)
60 — 'Le sept viellards'
61
62
63 — Dante Alighieri *Inferno* (early 14th century) Canto III
64 — Canto IV
65
66
67 — Saint Mary Woolnoth Church, London, England
68
69
70 — Battle in the First Punic War between Rome and Carthage (206BC)
71
72
73
74 — John Webster *The White Devil* (1612)
75
76 — Charles Baudelaire *Les Fleurs du Mal* (1857) 'Au Lecteur', French

II. A GAME OF CHESS

TITLE
77
78 — Thomas Middleton *A Game Of Chess* (1625); *Women Beware Women* (1657)
79
80
81
82 — William Shakespeare *Antony And Cleopatra* (c. 1603–07)
83
84 — Act II Scene II;
85 — *Cymbeline* (c. 1611)
86 — Act II Scene IV
87
88
89
90
91
92 — Virgil *Aeneid* (c. 29–19BC) Book 1
93
94
95
96
97 — John Milton *Paradise Lost* (1667)
98 — Book IV
99 — Ovid *Metamorphoses* (AD8)
100 — Tereus and Philomela
101
102
103 — Elizabethan onomatopoeic convention
104
105
106
107
108
109
110
111
112 — Vivienne Haigh-Wood Eliot's first wife
113
114
115
116
117
118 — John Webster *The White Devil* (1612)
119
120
121
122
123
124 — William Shakespeare *The Tempest* (c. 1610–11)
125 — Act I Scene II
126
127
128 — 'That Shakespearian Rag' (1912) Lyrics: Gene Buck/Herman Ruby Music: Dave Stamper
129
130
131
132
133
134

135
136
137
138 — Thomas Middleton *Women Beware Women* (1657)
139 — World War I (1914–18)
140
141 — Closing time announced at a pub
142
143
144
145
146
147
148
149
150
151
152 — Closing time announced at a pub
153
154
155 — Gossip from the Eliots' maid, Ellen Kellond
156
157
158
159
160
161
162
163
164
165 — Closing time announced at a pub
166
167
168
169 — Closing time announced at a pub
170
171 — William Shakespeare *Hamlet* (c. 1599–1602)
172 — Act IV Scene V

CATEGORIES BY COLOUR

- Post-14th-century literature
- Mythology and antiquity
- Religion
- Personal anecdotes
- Actual places
- Academic writing
- Art
- Major historical events
- Popular culture and traditions
- Eliot's earlier poems
- Other languages

T.S. ELIOT'S **THE WASTE LAND**

A subjective graphic interpretation of the allusions, references and hidden meanings in every line of T.S. Eliot's five-part epic poem, The Waste Land (1922).

III. THE FIRE SERMON

TITLE

173 — Buddha, The Fire Sermon
174
175 Edmund Spenser
176 *Prothalamion* (1596)
177 The River Thames
178
179
180 The Bible, Psalm 137;
181 Lake Geneva, where Eliot
182 worked on *The Waste Land*
183 while on rest-cure
184
185 Andrew Marvell
186 *To His Coy Mistress* (c. 1650s)
187
188
189
190 William Shakespeare
191 *The Tempest* (c. 1610–11)
192 Act I Scene II
193
194
195 John Day
196 *The Parliament Of Bees*
197 (c. 1608–16);
198 Diana and Actaeon
199 Ballad of unknown origin
200 Reported to Eliot in
201 Sydney, Australia
202 Paul Verlaine, *Parsifal* (1888);
203 Richard Wagner, *Parsifal* (1877)
204 Holy Grail, French
205 Tereus and Philomela
206 Charles Baudelaire
207 *Les Fleurs Du Mal* (1857)
208 'Le sept viellards'
209 Smyrna, Turkey focus of the
210 Greco-Turkish War (1919–22)
211 Trading abbreviation from
212 Eliot's time at Lloyds Bank
213 Cannon Street Hotel,
214 London, England
215 Metropole Hotel,
216 Brighton, England
217
218
219
220
221 — Sappho Fragment 149 (7BC)
222
223 Tiresias
224
225
226
227
228
229
230
231
232
233
234 Manufacturing town
235 of Bradford, England
236
237
238
239
240
241 Sophocles
242 *Antigone*
243 (c. 442BC);
244 *Oedipus Rex*
245 (c. 429BC);
246 Homer *Odyssey*
247 (late 8th century BC)
248
249
250
251 Oliver Goldsmith
252 *The Vicar Of*
253 *Wakefield* (1762)
254
255 William Shakespeare
256 *The Tempest* (c. 1610–11)
257 Act I Scene II
258
259 Streets running parallel to
260 the River Thames, London

261
262
263 Ionic columns in the
264 Church of St Magnus
265 the Martyr, London,
266 England
267
268
269
270
271
272
273
274
275 The River Thames at
276 Greenwich, London, England
277 Richard Wagner, *Die*
278 *Götterdämmerung* (1874)
279 James Anthony Froude
280 *History Of England From The*
281 *Fall Of Wolsey To The Death*
282 *Of Elizabeth* (1850–70)
283
284
285
286
287
288
289
290
291 Dante Alighieri
292 *Purgatorio* (early
293 14th century), Canto V
294 Richmond and Kew,
295 London, England
296 Moorgate, London,
297 England
298
299 Margate, where Eliot
300 worked on *The Waste*
301 *Land* while on rest-cure
302
303
304
305
306 St Augustine *Confessions*
307 (AD397–398)
308 Buddha, The Fire Sermon
309
310
311

IV. DEATH BY WATER

TITLE
312
313
314
315 T.S. Eliot
316 *Dans Le Restaurant* (1920)
317
318
319
320
321

V. WHAT THE THUNDER SAID

TITLE
322
323
324
325
326
327
328
329
330
331
332 The Bible, Matthew 26–27
333
334
335
336
337
338
339
340
341
342
343
344

345 — The Bible, Matthew 26 27
346
347
348
349
350
351
352
353
354
355
356 Sound of the hermit-thrush that
357 Eliot heard in Quebec County
358
359
360
361 Sir Ernest Shackleton,
362 *South* (1919);
363 The Bible, Luke 24
364
365
366
367
368
369
370 Hermann Hesse
371 *Blick Ins Chaos* (1922);
372 Post-World War I Europe
373
374 Jerusalem, Athens, Alexandria
375 Vienna, London
376 Charles Baudelaire
377 *Les Fleurs du Mal* (1857)
378 'Le sept viellards'
379
380
381
382
383
384
385 Jessie L. Weston *From Ritual*
386 *To Romance* (1922)
387 The Perilous Chapel
388
389
390
391 French onomatopoeic
392 convention
393
394
395 — The Ganges River, India
396
397 — The Himalayas, Sanskrit
398
399
400
401 — Sanskrit
402
403 Dante Alighieri *Inferno*
404 (early 14th century) Canto V
405
406
407 John Webster
408 *The White Devil* (1612)
409
410
411 Dante Alighieri *Inferno*
412 (early 14th century)
413 Canto XXXIII; F.H. Bradley
414 *Appearance And Reality* (1893)
415
416 William Shakespeare
417 *Coriolanus* (c. 1605–08)
418 Coriolanus, Roman war hero
419
420
421 Jessie L. Weston
422 *From Ritual To Romance* (1922)
423 The Fisher King
424 The Bible, Isaiah 38:1
425 Nursery rhyme, 'London Bridge'
426 Dante Alighieri *Purgatorio* (early
427 14th century) Canto XXVI, Italian
428 *Pervigilium Veneris*, Latin;
429 Tereus and Philomela
430 Gerard de Nerval *El Desdichado*
431 (1854), French
432 Thomas Kyd *The Spanish*
433 *Tragedie* (1592)
     Brihadaranyaka Upanishad

Brihadaranyaka Upanishad, The Three Disciples

SHAKEN, STIRRED
AND SOZZLED

Vodka martini, 'shaken not stirred' – often said as part of a bad Sean Connery impersonation – is one of the most quotable lines from Bond. Yet Her Majesty's top secret agent's love of the bottle would leave him impotent and at death's door.

Bond would be classified in the **'higher risk'** of problem drinkers and would be at **high risk of liver damage, an early death and impotence**.

Daily units of alcohol

13	**Bond's** *average* daily drinking habit
12	
11	
10	
9	**Higher risk**
8	*(regular)* drinkers
7	
6	
5	**Increasing risk**
4	*(regular)* drinkers
3	**Lower risk**
2	*(irregular)*
1	drinkers

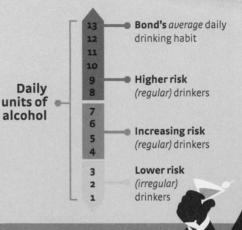

Doctors analyzing the Ian Fleming novels show James Bond polishes off the equivalent of **one and a half bottles of wine every day**.

They say he is **not the man to trust to deactivate a nuclear bomb**.

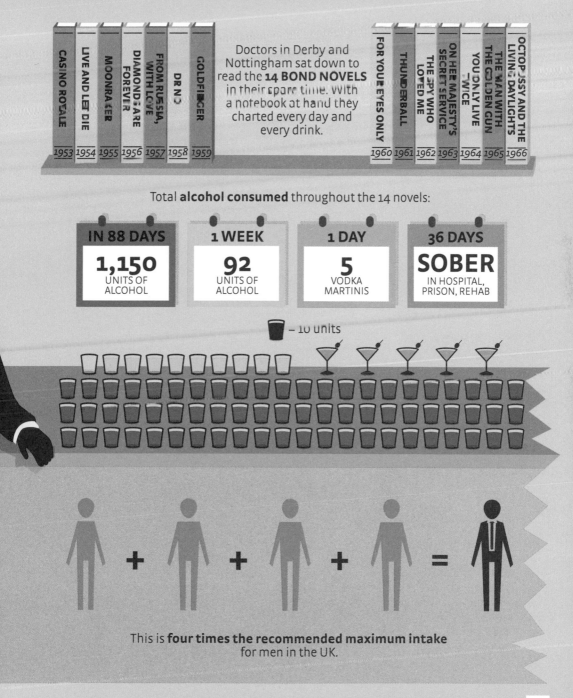

CASINO ROYALE · LIVE AND LET DIE · MOONRAKER · DIAMONDS ARE FOREVER · FROM RUSSIA, WITH LOVE · DR NO · GOLDFINGER

1953 1954 1955 1956 1957 1958 1959

Doctors in Derby and Nottingham sat down to read the **14 BOND NOVELS** in their spare time. With a notebook at hand they charted every day and every drink.

FOR YOUR EYES ONLY · THUNDERBALL · THE SPY WHO LOVED ME · ON HER MAJESTY'S SECRET SERVICE · YOU ONLY LIVE TWICE · THE MAN WITH THE GOLDEN GUN · OCTOPUSSY AND THE LIVING DAYLIGHTS

1960 1961 1962 1963 1964 1965 1966

Total **alcohol consumed** throughout the 14 novels:

IN 88 DAYS
1,150
UNITS OF ALCOHOL

1 WEEK
92
UNITS OF ALCOHOL

1 DAY
5
VODKA MARTINIS

36 DAYS
SOBER
IN HOSPITAL, PRISON, REHAB

– 10 units

This is **four times the recommended maximum intake** for men in the UK.

MOBY-DICK
BY NUMBERS

Moby-Dick; or, The Whale (1851) by former merchant seaman-turned-author Herman Melville was out of print when he died in 1891, aged 72, and his obituary in The New York Times misspelled the title. Yet it is now regarded as one of the greatest works of American fiction to have been written. It's a book as big as the white whale was described as being.

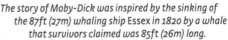

WHALE SIZE

Ishmael's calculations of the size of the largest sperm whale:
85–90ft long, 40ft circumference, weight 90 tons; 20 ribs, each from 6ft to 8ft long.

21st-century adult sperm whales:
measures between 49–59ft (15–18m) and weighs between 35–45 tonnes.

The story of Moby-Dick was inspired by the sinking of the 87ft (27m) whaling ship Essex *in 1820 by a whale that survivors claimed was 85ft (26m) long.*

Average price sperm whale meat and oil (1850):
£150 ($300) per whale

Price of ambergris:
1 gold guinea per ounce

THE BOOK

Number of words total: **209,117**

Number of chapters total: **135**

Shortest chapter: **#122** (Midnight, Aloft), **36 words**

Longest chapter: **#54** (The Town-Ho's Story), **7,938 words**

Number of chapters before casting off to sea: **21**

Number of chapters before Ahab appears: **27**

Number of chapters before Moby-Dick is sighted: **132**

THE STORY

Narrator and sole survivor of the voyage – **Ishmael**

Whaling ship for the voyage – **The *Pequod***

Captain of the *Pequod* – **Ahab** (58 years old)

Number of characters named after Biblical characters
(Ishmael from Genesis, Ahab and Elijah both from Books of Kings)

Number of crew members on the *Pequod*

Number of nationalities in the crew

Number of other whaling ships met during the voyage

Number of other whaling ships to sight Moby-Dick

Number of harpooners on the *Pequod*

Number of American harpooners on the *Pequod* (Tashtego)

Number of whales killed by the *Pequod* before meeting Moby-Dick

Number of multinational coffee chains named after a character in the book (Starbucks)

Number of whalers killed by Moby-Dick during the voyage not on the *Pequod*

Number of *Pequod* crew killed by Moby-Dick

Number of sea captains killed by Moby-Dick on the voyage

Number of limbs consumed by Moby-Dick

Number of limbs made out of whale bone

Number of garments made out of whale penis

HOW AN IDEA BECOMES **A BOOK**

In an effort to demystify the publishing business, here's how an idea can take one of five different routes to publication. Whether a first-time author, a best-selling writer, celebrity, hip website owner or a publisher originating the process in-house, these are the steps the process can take from the beginning to end.

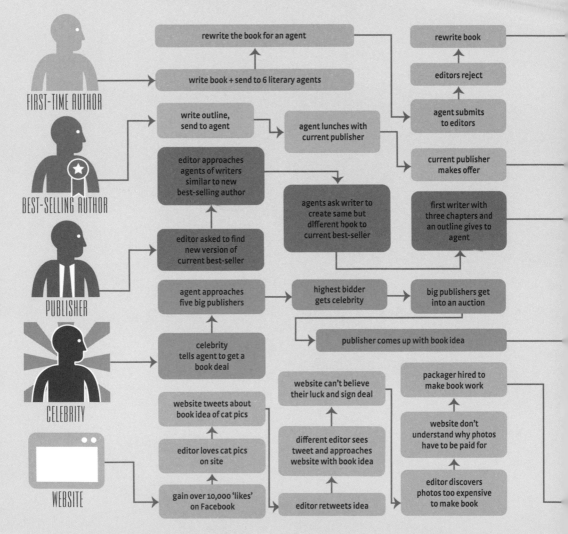

FIRST-TIME AUTHOR

BEST-SELLING AUTHOR

PUBLISHER

CELEBRITY

WEBSITE

rewrite the book for an agent

write book + send to 6 literary agents

rewrite book

editors reject

agent submits to editors

write outline, send to agent

agent lunches with current publisher

editor approaches agents of writers similar to new best-selling author

current publisher makes offer

agents ask writer to create same but different hook to current best-seller

first writer with three chapters and an outline gives to agent

editor asked to find new version of current best-seller

agent approaches five big publishers

highest bidder gets celebrity

big publishers get into an auction

celebrity tells agent to get a book deal

publisher comes up with book idea

website can't believe their luck and sign deal

packager hired to make book work

website tweets about book idea of cat pics

editor loves cat pics on site

different editor sees tweet and approaches website with book idea

website don't understand why photos have to be paid for

gain over 10,000 'likes' on Facebook

editor retweets idea

editor discovers photos too expensive to make book

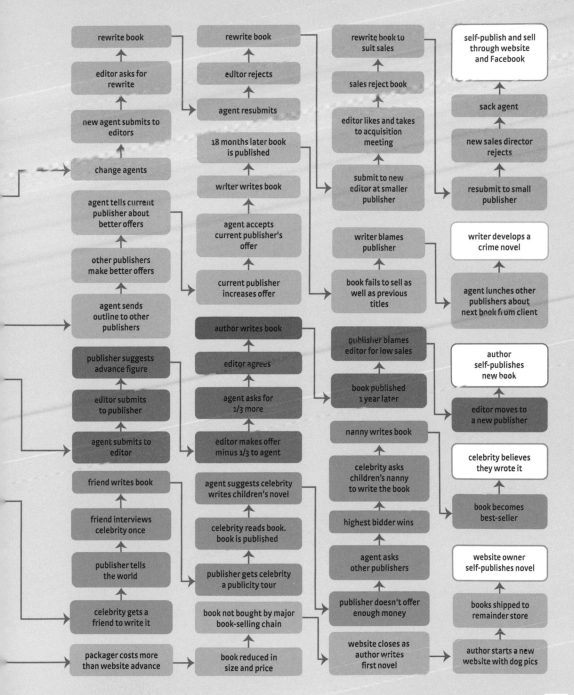

CITY **LITS**

When choosing a setting for a work of fiction, the choice of city can determine what kind of story the author is embarking upon. Some cities have so many disparate styles of story set in them that they have an anomalous meaning, but these six have become representative of a particular style of fiction.

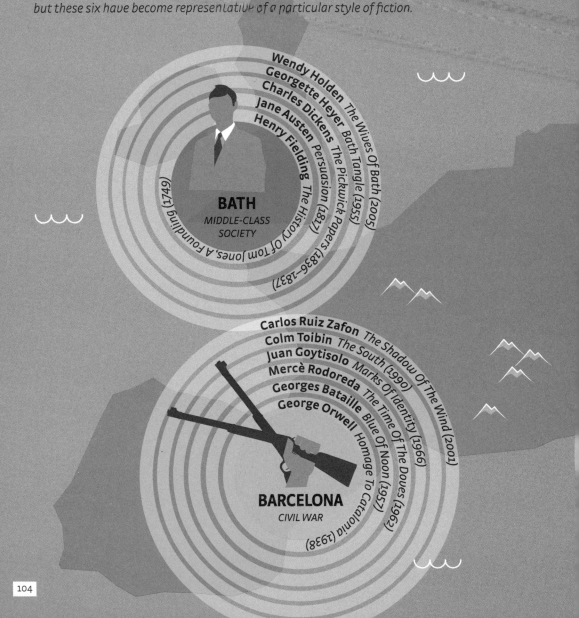

BATH
MIDDLE-CLASS
SOCIETY

Wendy Holden *The Wives Of Bath* (2005)
Georgette Heyer *Bath Tangle* (1955)
Charles Dickens *The Pickwick Papers* (1836–1837)
Jane Austen *Persuasion* (1817)
Henry Fielding *The History Of Tom Jones, A Foundling* (1749)

BARCELONA
CIVIL WAR

Carlos Ruiz Zafon *The Shadow Of The Wind* (2001)
Colm Toibin *The South* (1990)
Juan Goytisolo *Marks Of Identity* (1966)
Mercè Rodoreda *The Time Of The Doves* (1962)
Georges Bataille *Blue Of Noon* (1957)
George Orwell *Homage To Catalonia* (1938)

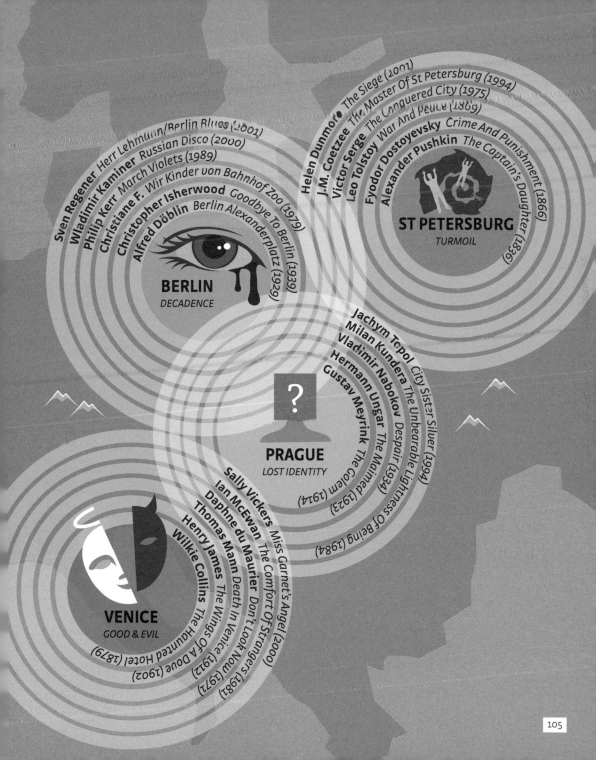

BERLIN
DECADENCE

Sven Regener *Herr Lehmann/Berlin Blues (2001)*
Wladimir Kaminer *Russian Disco (2000)*
Philip Kerr *March Violets (1989)*
Christiane F. *Wir Kinder von Bahnhof Zoo (1979)*
Christopher Isherwood *Goodbye To Berlin (1939)*
Alfred Döblin *Berlin Alexanderplatz (1929)*

ST PETERSBURG
TURMOIL

Helen Dunmore *The Siege (2001)*
J.M. Coetzee *The Master Of St Petersburg (1994)*
Victor Serge *The Conquered City (1975)*
Leo Tolstoy *War And Peace (1869)*
Fyodor Dostoyevsky *Crime And Punishment (1866)*
Alexander Pushkin *The Captain's Daughter (1836)*

PRAGUE
LOST IDENTITY

Jachym Topol *City Sister Silver (1994)*
Milan Kundera *The Unbearable Lightness Of Being (1984)*
Vladimir Nabokov *Despair (1934)*
Hermann Ungar *The Maimed (1923)*
Gustav Meyrink *The Golem (1914)*

VENICE
GOOD & EVIL

Sally Vickers *Miss Garnet's Angel (2000)*
Ian McEwan *The Comfort Of Strangers (1981)*
Daphne du Maurier *Don't Look Now (1971)*
Thomas Mann *Death In Venice (1912)*
Henry James *The Wings Of A Dove (1902)*
Wilkie Collins *The Haunted Hotel (1879)*

LITERARY
CUTS

Guess the female author from her hairstyle.

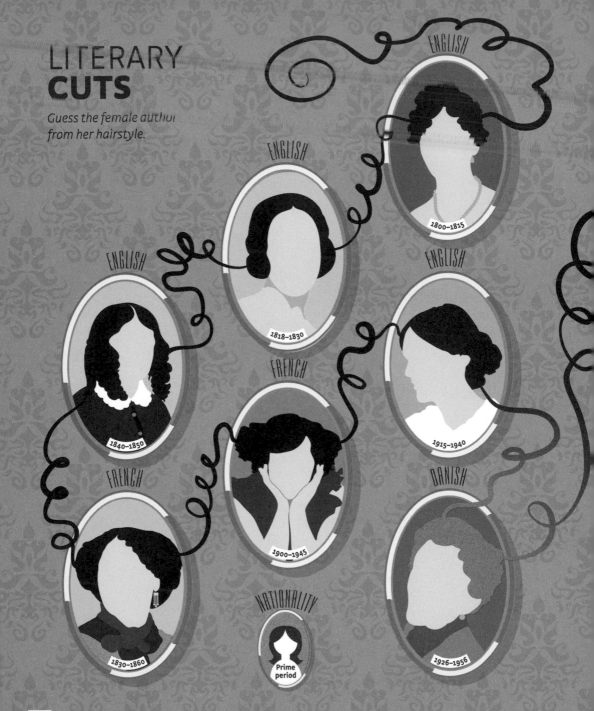

ENGLISH
1800–1815

ENGLISH
1818–1830

ENGLISH
1840–1850

ENGLISH
1915–1940

FRENCH
1900–1945

FRENCH
1830–1860

NATIONALITY

Prime period

DANISH
1926–1956

FRENCH

AMERICAN

ENGLISH

1940–1970

1970–1980

AMERICAN

1950–1990

AMERICAN

1992–2013

GERMAN-ROMANIAN

1980–2000

ENGLISH

ENGLISH

1997–2007

1980–2000

2011–2013

THE **GROWLERY**

Dogs have always been much more useful to man than cats; as a hunting aid, a source of heat and energy, and a guard against attack. It's little wonder that stories involving canine characters stretch back to the pre-Greek era. In this handy dog matrix, the four aspects of doggy behaviour attest to the versatility of the species as a literary device.

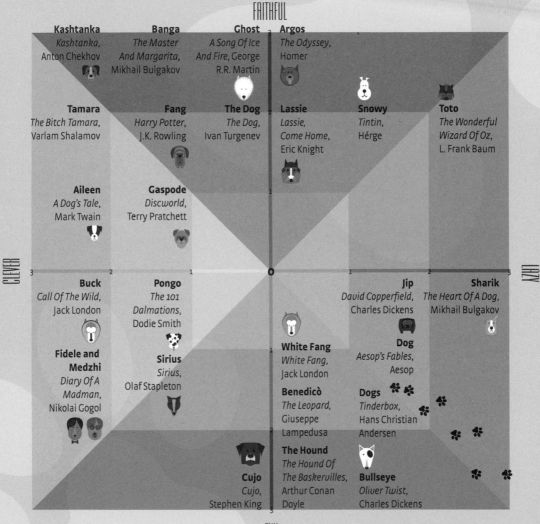

FAITHFUL

Kashtanka
Kashtanka,
Anton Chekhov

Banga
The Master And Margarita,
Mikhail Bulgakov

Ghost
A Song Of Ice And Fire, George R.R. Martin

Argos
The Odyssey,
Homer

Tamara
The Bitch Tamara,
Varlam Shalamov

Fang
Harry Potter,
J.K. Rowling

The Dog
The Dog,
Ivan Turgenev

Lassie
Lassie, Come Home,
Eric Knight

Snowy
Tintin,
Hérge

Toto
The Wonderful Wizard Of Oz,
L. Frank Baum

Aileen
A Dog's Tale,
Mark Twain

Gaspode
Discworld,
Terry Pratchett

CLEVER 3 2 1 0 1 2 3 MEAN

Buck
Call Of The Wild,
Jack London

Pongo
The 101 Dalmations,
Dodie Smith

Jip
David Copperfield,
Charles Dickens

Sharik
The Heart Of A Dog,
Mikhail Bulgakov

Fidele and Medzhi
Diary Of A Madman,
Nikolai Gogol

Sirius
Sirius,
Olaf Stapleton

White Fang
White Fang,
Jack London

Dog
Aesop's Fables,
Aesop

Benedicò
The Leopard,
Giuseppe Lampedusa

Dogs
Tinderbox,
Hans Christian Andersen

The Hound
The Hound Of The Baskervilles,
Arthur Conan Doyle

Bullseye
Oliver Twist,
Charles Dickens

Cujo
Cujo,
Stephen King

EVIL

AGE SHALL NOT WITHER THEM

While poets have been published at an early age (Neruda was 14, Rimbaud 15, Walcott 18), the average age of debut novelists is in their 30s. Which makes these youngest and oldest debut novelists truly exceptional.

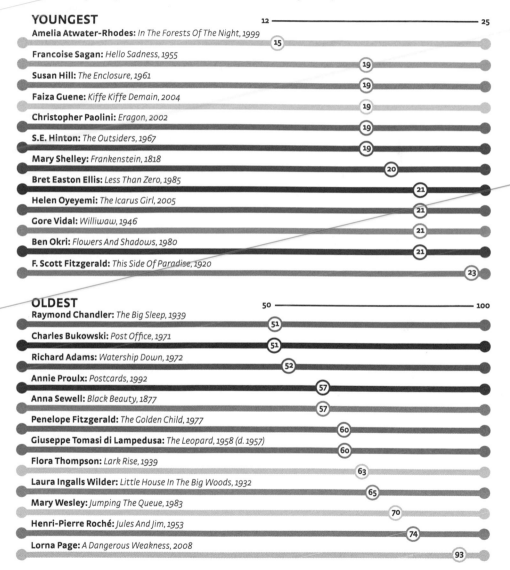

YOUNGEST

12 ———————————————————————— 25

Amelia Atwater-Rhodes: *In The Forests Of The Night, 1999* — 15

Francoise Sagan: *Hello Sadness, 1955* — 19

Susan Hill: *The Enclosure, 1961* — 19

Faiza Guene: *Kiffe Kiffe Demain, 2004* — 19

Christopher Paolini: *Eragon, 2002* — 19

S.E. Hinton: *The Outsiders, 1967* — 19

Mary Shelley: *Frankenstein, 1818* — 20

Bret Easton Ellis: *Less Than Zero, 1985* — 21

Helen Oyeyemi: *The Icarus Girl, 2005* — 21

Gore Vidal: *Williwaw, 1946* — 21

Ben Okri: *Flowers And Shadows, 1980* — 21

F. Scott Fitzgerald: *This Side Of Paradise, 1920* — 23

OLDEST

50 ———————————————————————— 100

Raymond Chandler: *The Big Sleep, 1939* — 51

Charles Bukowski: *Post Office, 1971* — 51

Richard Adams: *Watership Down, 1972* — 52

Annie Proulx: *Postcards, 1992* — 57

Anna Sewell: *Black Beauty, 1877* — 57

Penelope Fitzgerald: *The Golden Child, 1977* — 60

Giuseppe Tomasi di Lampedusa: *The Leopard, 1958 (d. 1957)* — 60

Flora Thompson: *Lark Rise, 1939* — 63

Laura Ingalls Wilder: *Little House In The Big Woods, 1932* — 65

Mary Wesley: *Jumping The Queue, 1983* — 70

Henri-Pierre Roché: *Jules And Jim, 1953* — 74

Lorna Page: *A Dangerous Weakness, 2008* — 93

TRANSLATOR · POET · PHILOSOPHER · JOURNALIST · ESSAYIST · DRAMATIST · AUTHOR

Hildegard of Bingen · Julian of Norwich · Margery Kempe · Elizabeth Cary · Mary Sidney · Anne Askew · Anne Lock · Aphra Behn · Mary Pix · Susanna Centlivre · Mary Wollstonecraft · Eliza Haywood · Frances Sheridan · Caroline Schlegel · Mary Shelley · Harriet Beecher Stowe · George Eliot · Jane Austen · Annette von Droste-Hülshoff · Charlotte Brontë · Emily Brontë · Anne Brontë · Selma Lagerlöf · Ricarda Huch · Willa Cather · Radclyffe Hall · Edith Wharton · Elizabeth Barrett Browning · Emily Dickinson · Karen Blixen · Simone de Beauvoir · Virginia Woolf · Astrid Lindgren · Iris Murdoch · Margaret Atwood

A ROOM OF **ONE'S OWN**

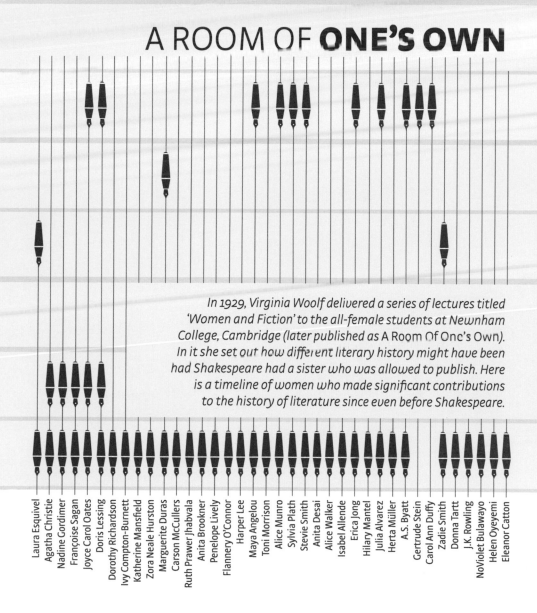

In 1929, Virginia Woolf delivered a series of lectures titled
'Women and Fiction' to the all-female students at Newnham
College, Cambridge (later published as A Room Of One's Own).
In it she set out how different literary history might have been
had Shakespeare had a sister who was allowed to publish. Here
is a timeline of women who made significant contributions
to the history of literature since even before Shakespeare.

Laura Esquivel
Agatha Christie
Nadine Gordimer
Françoise Sagan
Joyce Carol Oates
Doris Lessing
Dorothy Richardson
Ivy Compton-Burnett
Katherine Mansfield
Zora Neale Hurston
Marguerite Duras
Carson McCullers
Ruth Prawer Jhabvala
Anita Brookner
Penelope Lively
Flannery O'Connor
Harper Lee
Maya Angelou
Toni Morrison
Alice Munro
Sylvia Plath
Stevie Smith
Anita Desai
Alice Walker
Isabel Allende
Erica Jong
Hilary Mantel
Julia Alvarez
Herta Müller
A.S. Byatt
Gertrude Stein
Carol Ann Duffy
Zadie Smith
Donna Tartt
J.K. Rowling
NoViolet Bulawayo
Helen Oyeyemi
Eleanor Catton

DULCE ET **DECORUM EST**

There were soldier authors who fought, wrote and died in the trenches of World War I. Among them were novelists, playwrights and poets, some of whom perished not in battle, but years later. They will always be remembered for the work they wrote about the experiences of war, whatever side of no man's land they stood.

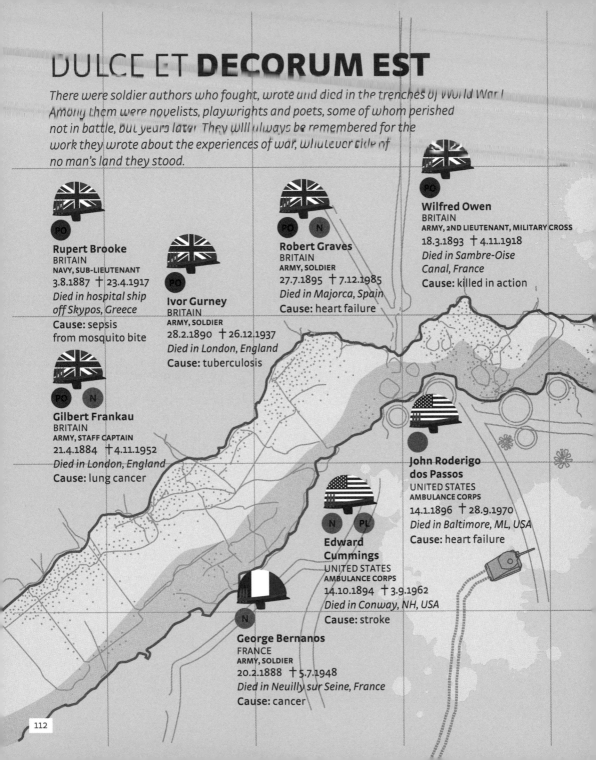

Wilfred Owen
BRITAIN
ARMY, 2ND LIEUTENANT, MILITARY CROSS
18.3.1893 † 4.11.1918
Died in Sambre-Oise Canal, France
Cause: killed in action

Rupert Brooke
BRITAIN
NAVY, SUB-LIEUTENANT
3.8.1887 † 23.4.1917
Died in hospital ship off Skypos, Greece
Cause: sepsis from mosquito bite

Ivor Gurney
BRITAIN
ARMY, SOLDIER
28.2.1890 † 26.12.1937
Died in London, England
Cause: tuberculosis

Robert Graves
BRITAIN
ARMY, SOLDIER
27.7.1895 † 7.12.1985
Died in Majorca, Spain
Cause: heart failure

Gilbert Frankau
BRITAIN
ARMY, STAFF CAPTAIN
21.4.1884 † 4.11.1952
Died in London, England
Cause: lung cancer

John Roderigo dos Passos
UNITED STATES
AMBULANCE CORPS
14.1.1896 † 28.9.1970
Died in Baltimore, ML, USA
Cause: heart failure

Edward Cummings
UNITED STATES
AMBULANCE CORPS
14.10.1894 † 3.9.1962
Died in Conway, NH, USA
Cause: stroke

George Bernanos
FRANCE
ARMY, SOLDIER
20.2.1888 † 5.7.1948
Died in Neuilly sur Seine, France
Cause: cancer

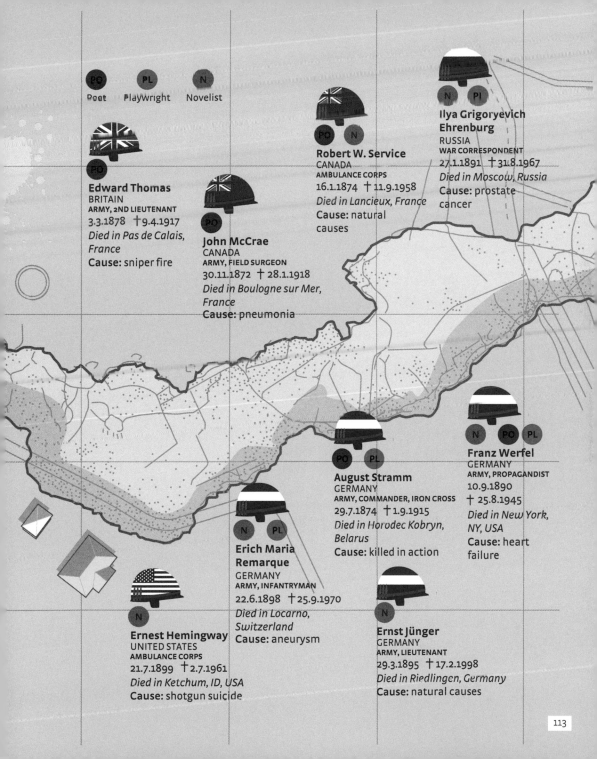

PO Poet PL Playwright N Novelist

Edward Thomas
BRITAIN
ARMY, 2ND LIEUTENANT
3.3.1878 †9.4.1917
Died in Pas de Calais, France
Cause: sniper fire

John McCrae
CANADA
ARMY, FIELD SURGEON
30.11.1872 †28.1.1918
Died in Boulogne sur Mer, France
Cause: pneumonia

Robert W. Service
CANADA
AMBULANCE CORPS
16.1.1874 †11.9.1958
Died in Lancieux, France
Cause: natural causes

Ilya Grigoryevich Ehrenburg
RUSSIA
WAR CORRESPONDENT
27.1.1891 †31.8.1967
Died in Moscow, Russia
Cause: prostate cancer

August Stramm
GERMANY
ARMY, COMMANDER, IRON CROSS
29.7.1874 †1.9.1915
Died in Horodec Kobryn, Belarus
Cause: killed in action

Franz Werfel
GERMANY
ARMY, PROPAGANDIST
10.9.1890 † 25.8.1945
Died in New York, NY, USA
Cause: heart failure

Erich Maria Remarque
GERMANY
ARMY, INFANTRYMAN
22.6.1898 †25.9.1970
Died in Locarno, Switzerland
Cause: aneurysm

Ernest Hemingway
UNITED STATES
AMBULANCE CORPS
21.7.1899 †2.7.1961
Died in Ketchum, ID, USA
Cause: shotgun suicide

Ernst Jünger
GERMANY
ARMY, LIEUTENANT
29.3.1895 †17.2.1998
Died in Riedlingen, Germany
Cause: natural causes

NOSTALGIA
IS WHAT IT
USED TO BE

The Color Purple
Alice Walker

Roots
Alex Hayley

Gone With The Wind
Margaret Mitchell

Treasure Island
Robert Louis Stevenson

War And Peace
Leo Tolstoy

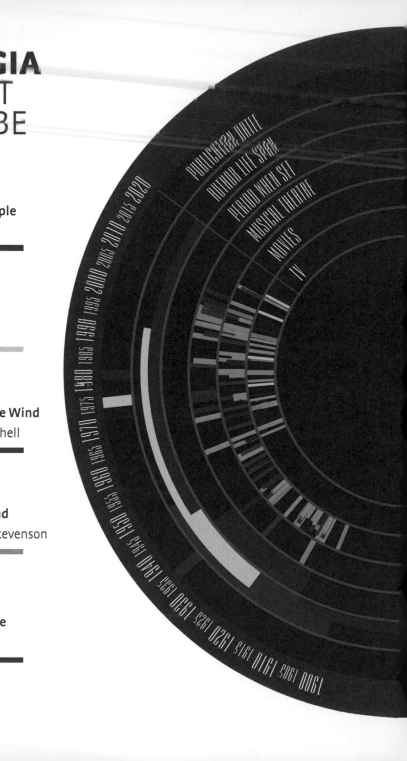

PUBLICATION DATE
AUTHOR LIFE SPAN
PERIOD WHEN SET
MUSICAL THEATRE
MOVIES
TV

1900 1905 1910 1915 1920 1925 1930 1935 1940 1945 1950 1955 1960 1965 1970 1975 1980 1985 1990 1995 2000 2005 2010 2015 2020

1190
1400
1700
1750
1800
1805
1810
1815
1820
1825
1830
1835
1840
1845
1850
1855
1860
1865
1870
1875
1880
1885
1890
1895

Ivanhoe
Walter Scott

The Hunchback Of Notre-Dame
Victor Hugo

The Three Musketeers
Alexandre Dumas

Vanity Fair
William Makepeace Thackeray

A Tale Of Two Cities
Charles Dickens

DEATH IN DISCWORLD

The character of Death has appeared in all but two of the 40 books written by Terry Pratchett in the Discworld series between 1983 and 2013. There are five titles in which Death is the central character. As with all Pratchett's work, they are filled with allusions and references beyond the obvious. Here's what each one is really about

Number of allusions referenced ?

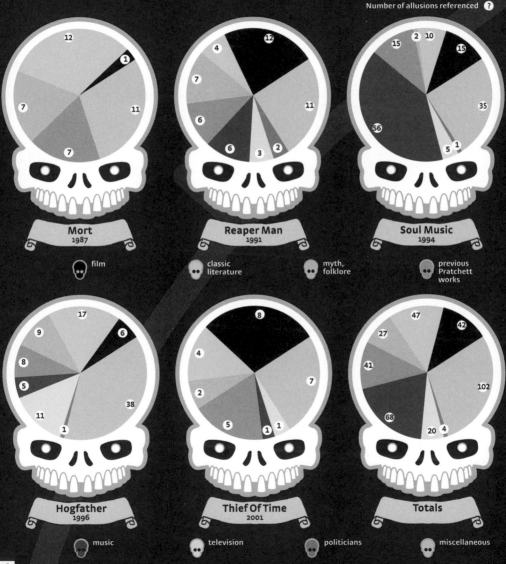

Mort
1987

Reaper Man
1991

Soul Music
1994

- film
- classic literature
- myth, folklore
- previous Pratchett works

Hogfather
1996

Thief Of Time
2001

Totals

- music
- television
- politicians
- miscellaneous

ON THE **SONNET***

The most popular sonnet form was first used by a now little-read Italian poet named Jacopo da Lentini, circa 1210–1260. After his 14-line format was adopted by countrymen Dante Alighieri and Petrarch in the following century, the sonnet as we know it became a staple of poetry. Here, in 14 poets and one of their key works laid out in rhyme schemes, is a history of the sonnet from 1266–2013.

POET (DATES)	KEY SONNET (DATE)	NATIONALITY
Dante Alighieri 1266–1321	*A Casan'alma Presa e Gentil Core* 1295	ITALIAN
Petrarch 1304–1874	*Una Candida Cerva* 1368	ITALIAN
Thomas Wyatt 1503–1542	*Whoso List To Hunt* 1536–1540	ENGLISH
William Shakespeare 1564–1616	*Sonnet #18, Shall I Compare Thee To A Summer's Day?* 1609	ENGLISH
John Donne 1572–1631	*Holy Sonnet #10, Death Be Not Proud* 1633	ENGLISH
John Milton 1608–1674	*When I Consider How My Light Is Spent* 1652	ENGLISH
William Wordsworth 1770–1850	*The World Is Too Much With Us* 1802–1804	ENGLISH
Percy Bysshe Shelley 1792–1822	*Ozymandias* 1817	ENGLISH
Charles Baudelaire 1821–1867	*Autumn Sonnet* 1857	FRENCH
Dante Gabriel Rossetti 1828–1882	*A Sonnet (From The House Of Life)* 1870	ENGLISH
Rainer Maria Rilke 1875–1926	*Die Sonneten An Orpheus #29* 1922	GERMAN
Edna St Vincent Millay 1892–1950	*I, Being Born A Woman And Distressed* 1923	AMERICAN
Pablo Neruda 1904–1973	*100 Love Sonnets #17* 1959	ARGENTINIAN
Seamus Heaney 1939–2013	*A Dream Of Jealousy* 1979	IRISH

RHYME SCHEME

A ▲   B ♥   C ●   D ◗   E ■   F ✚   G ◿   H ◆   I ▮   J ✓   K ✦   L (M ❖   N ✖

BOOKS FOR COOKS

Not all books with recipes in them have been written by celebrity chefs. Some have been penned by the greatest novelists and playwrights in the world, as this menu of dishes taken from numerous titles proves.

1397 · MENU · 1977

SOUPS

- Borscht — 1933
- Clam chowder with pounded ship's biscuits — 1851
- Soupe à la tortue à la Louisianne *(Turtle soup)* — 1958

STARTERS

- Omelette with biscuits — 1869
- Avocado pear stuffed with crabmeat and mayonnaise — 1963
- Pickled herring *(Twelfth Night)* — 1602
- Crayfish — 1933
- Partridge wing *(Much Ado About Nothing)* — 1599
- Cold chicken slices — 1963
- Salted pork flakes in butter — 1851
- Spiced beef jellies — 1913
- Hot venison pasty *(The Merry Wives Of Windsor)* — 1602

MAINS

PORK

- Gammon of bacon *(Henry IV Part 1)* — 1597
- Bacon and ham — 1820

BEEF

- Corned beef and potatoes — 1869
- Beef and mustard *(The Taming Of The Shrew)* — 1592
- Beef with stewed plums — 1933
- Rare roast beef — 1963

LAMB

- Joint of mutton *(Henry IV Part 2)* — 1599

CHICKEN & GAME

- Chicken en casserole — 1933
- Pigeon pie — 1820
- Quails in coffins — *1958*
- Duck with onion sauce — 1820
- Roasted crane — c.1387

FISH & SEAFOOD

- Fish poached in white wine, capers and sorrels — 1977

SPECIALS OF THE DAY

MONDAY
Blankmanger   c.1387
*(rice boiled in almond milk,
with chunks of chicken or fish)*

TUESDAY
Blinis Demidof a l'Oobleck   1958

WEDNESDAY
Jakke of Dover   c.1387
*(stale meat or fish pie/pasty, dressed in
blood or gravy to make it appear fresh)*

THURSDAY
Broil'd tripe   1592
(The Taming Of The Shrew)

FRIDAY
Whale steak   1851

• HOUSE SPECIALITIES •

A DOZEN OYSTERS
1933

BLACK CAVIAR
1963

LOBSTER
1869

SIDES

Bread rubbed with garlic   1933
Sop *(toasted bread or cake
dipped in wine)*   c.1387
Wastel-breed *(fine white bread)*   c.1387
Garleek, oynons and lekes   c.1387
Asparagus (with butter)   1869/1913
New potatoes   1913/1933
Mustard gratin   1977
Stewed tripe   1977

MENU KEY

● *The Canterbury Tales* Geoffrey Chaucer (1387–1400)

● *The Complete Works Of Shakespeare*
William Shakespeare (c.1590–1613)

● *The Legend Of Sleepy Hollow* Washington Irving (1820)

● *Moby Dick* Herman Melville (1851)

● *Little Women* Louisa May Alcott (1868–69)

● *In Search Of Lost Time* Marcel Proust (1913)

● *Down And Out In Paris And London*
George Orwell (1933)

● *Babette's Feast* Isak Dinesen (1958)

● *The Bell Jar* Sylvia Plath (1963)

● *The Flounder* Günter Grass (1977)

DESSERTS

Stewed prunes   1602
(The Merry Wives Of Windsor)
Buttered slapjacks (pancakes)   1820
with honey
Blancmange and strawberries   1869
Madeleines   1913
Cherry tartlets shaped like boats   1913
Chocolate cake   1913
Sweet pudding   1933
Roquefort cheese   1933
Marzipan fruit   1963

BEVERAGES

BEERS
Bragot *(drink of fermented ale,
honey and spices)*   c.1387
A jubbe of London ale   c.1387

WINES
Vernage *(sweet Italian wine)*   c.1387
Wyn   c.1387
Ypocras *(spiced wine)*   c.1387

godecookery.com, finedininglovers.com, pbs.org, foodrepublic.com, literaryfoodporn.blogspot.co.uk

THANKS, BUT **NO THANKS**

To be awarded a major prize for anything is usually considered to be a crowning achievement. However there have been 15 authors who refused major prizes for their work (or refused nominations); here's who they were, and why they said 'thanks, but no thanks'.

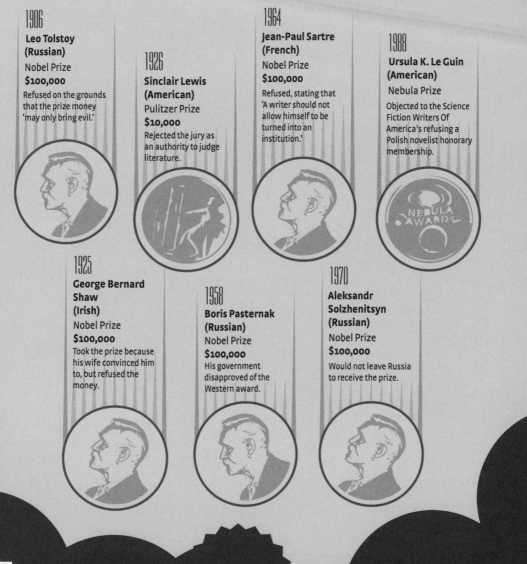

1906
Leo Tolstoy (Russian)
Nobel Prize
$100,000
Refused on the grounds that the prize money 'may only bring evil.'

1926
Sinclair Lewis (American)
Pulitzer Prize
$10,000
Rejected the jury as an authority to judge literature.

1964
Jean-Paul Sartre (French)
Nobel Prize
$100,000
Refused, stating that 'A writer should not allow himself to be turned into an institution.'

1988
Ursula K. Le Guin (American)
Nebula Prize
Objected to the Science Fiction Writers Of America's refusing a Polish novelist honorary membership.

1925
George Bernard Shaw (Irish)
Nobel Prize
$100,000
Took the prize because his wife convinced him to, but refused the money.

1958
Boris Pasternak (Russian)
Nobel Prize
$100,000
His government disapproved of the Western award.

1970
Aleksandr Solzhenitsyn (Russian)
Nobel Prize
$100,000
Would not leave Russia to receive the prize.

2003

**Hari Kunzru
(English)**

John Llewellyn Rhys Prize
$8,400 (£5,000)

Objected to the xenophobic views of prize's sponsor, the Mail On Sunday

2006

**Peter Handke
(Austrian)**

Heinrich Heine German Literature Prize
$68,500 (€50,000)

Accepted then rejected the prize after German politicians opposed his perceived support of Slobodan Milosevic

2011

**Michael Ondaatje
(Sri Lankan-Canadian)**

Scotiabank Giller Prize

Thought that he had received it too many times already, and should not enter again.

2008

**Adolf Muschg
(German)**

Swiss Book Prize
$68,500 (€50,000)

Compared the prize to a TV reality show spectacle and said he didn't write for that kind of reception.

2011

**John Le Carré
(English)**

Man Booker Prize
$81,000 (£50,000)

Refused nomination because he doesn't believe in competing for literary awards.

2011

**Alice Oswald
(English),
John Kinsella
(Australian)**

Poetry Book Society T.S. Eliot Prize
$25,000 (£15,000)

Declined nomination because of a sponsorship deal with an investment company.

2012

**Javier Marías
(Spanish)**

Spanish National Narrative Prize
$27,400 (€20,000)

Prize is state-funded and he is against receiving public money.

2012

**Lawrence Ferlinghetti
(American)**

Pannonius Prize
$68,500 (€50,000)

Because the award is funded in part by the repressive Hungarian government.

Upper West Side

Time-travelling advertising artist meets a promiscuous college teacher

Simon Morley of Jack Finney's *Time And Again* meets **Theresa Dunn** of Judith Rossner's *Looking For Mr Goodbar*

Harlem

Con-man using black politics meets invisible man born of black politics

Deke O'Hara of Chester Himes' *Cotton Comes To Harlem* meets the **unnamed narrator** of Ralph Ellison's *Invisible Man*

Central Park

Teenage rebel meets self-absorbed flapper

Holden Caulfield of J.D. Salinger's *Catcher In The Rye* meets **Daisy Buchanan** of F. Scott Fitzgerald's *The Great Gatsby*

Greenwich Village

Suicidal jazz drummer meets depressed journalist

Rufus Scott of James Baldwin's *Another Country* meets **Esther Greenwood** of Sylvia Plath's *The Bell Jar*

Washington Square

Shy, plain reluctant heiress with overbearing father meets reluctant heir with overbearing father

Catherine Sloper of Henry James' *Washington Square* meets **Mike Corleone** of Mario Puzo's *The Godfather*

Wall Street

Stock Exchange terrorist meets self-styled Master Of The Universe

Lyle of Don DeLillo's *Players* meets **Sherman McCoy** of Tom Wolfe's *Bonfire Of The Vanities*

Lower Manhattan

Lonely rich businessman meets lonely rich music label owner

George Smith of J.P. Donleavy's *A Singular Man* meets **Bennie Salazar** from Jennifer Egan's *A Visit From The Goon Squad*

Lower Broadway

architect supremacist meets reluctant sleuth

Howard Roark of Ayn Rand's *The Fountainhead* meets **Nick Charles** of Dashiell Hammett's *The Thin Man*

Fifth Avenue

Fantasizing society girl meets fantasizing counters

Holly Golightly of Truman Capote's *Breakfast At Tiffany's* meets **Countess Ellen Olenska** of Edith Wharton's *The Age Of Innocence*

Lexington

Murderous amoral investment banker meets avenging amoral vigilante

Patrick Bateman of Bret Easton Ellis' *American Psycho* meets **Rorschach** of *Watchmen*

Empire State Building

Frustrated vengeful Jewish refugee meets frustrated vengeful Jewish immigrant

Josef 'Joe' Kavalier of Michael Chabon's *Kavalier & Clay* meets **David Schearl** of Henry Roth's *Call It Sleep*

Williamsburg

Orthodox Jewish teenage math genius meets book-loving Jewish teen

Reuven Malter of Chaim Potok's *The Chosen* meets **Francie Nolan** of Betty Smith's *A Tree Grows In Brooklyn*

Midtown

Egotistical actress meets abused Macy's assistant

Neely of Jacqueline Susan's *Valley Of The Dolls* meets **Kay Strong** of Mary McCarthy's *The Group*

Brooklyn

Private investigator with Tourette's Syndrome meets transvestite prostitute

Essrog of Jonathan Letham's *Motherless Brooklyn* meets **Georgette** of Hubert Selby Jr's *Last Exit To Brooklyn*

East Broadway

Nine-year-old with a dead dad meets lonely old man with imaginary friend

Oskar Schell of Jonathan Safran Foer's *Extremely Loud And Incredibly Close* meets **Leo Gursky** of Nicole Krauss' *The History Of Love*

Brooklyn Heights

Fictional fiction author meets concentration camp survivor

Daniel Quinn of Paul Auster's *New York Trilogy* meets **Sophie Zawistowska** of William Styron's *Sophie's Choice*

Lower East Side

Morally challenged bar manager meets morally challenged copy-editor

Eric Cash of Richard Price's *Lush Life* meets **Asa Leventhal** of Saul Bellow's *The Victim*

MEET ME IN
NEW YORK

Imagining the literary characters of different centuries and authors meeting at the great locations of New York where their stories are set.

IN MEMORIAM
A.H.H.

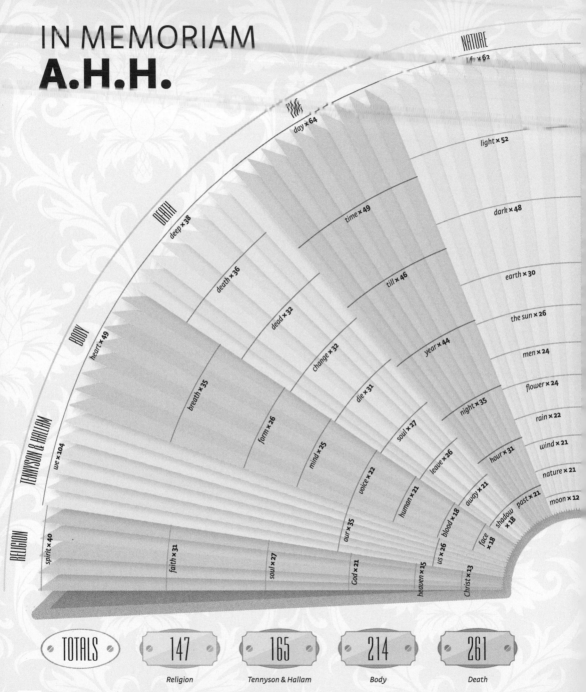

NATURE — life × 62

TIME — day × 64

DEATH — deep × 38

BODY — heart × 49

TENNYSON & HALLAM — we × 104

RELIGION — spirit × 40

light × 52
dark × 48
earth × 30
the sun × 26
men × 24
flower × 24
rain × 22
wind × 21
nature × 21
moon × 12

time × 49
till × 46
year × 44
night × 35
hour × 31
away × 21
past × 21
shadow × 18
face × 18

death × 36
dead × 32
change × 32
die × 31
soul × 27
leave × 26
blood × 18

breath × 35
form × 26
mind × 25
voice × 22
human × 21
us × 26

faith × 31
soul × 27
God × 21
heaven × 35
Christ × 13
our × 35

TOTALS

147	165	214	261
Religion	Tennyson & Hallam	Body	Death

124

SENSIBILITY

(love/loved) × 159

Alfred Lord Tennyson's elegiac poem 'In Memoriam A.H.H.' was published in 1849, after 17 years of composition. The 133 cantos were written for a former Cambridge University friend of the poet, Arthur Henry Hallam, who died of a brain haemorrhage aged 22. As this graphic shows, Tennyson writes predominantly of himself and Hallam, with religion a long way behind other concerns.

TENNYSON

I × 290

HALLAM

thou × 136

thy × 113

he × 105

his × 92

thee × 84

thought × 30

sweet × 29

doubt × 25

grief × 22

sorrow × 22

calm × 18

feel × 17

joy × 13

passion × 7

me × 64

mine × 28

him × 75

thine × 23

290	342	342	382	628
Time	Nature	Sensibility	Tennyson	Hallam

DEGREES OF SEPARATION:
STEPHEN KING

At the height of his success, best-selling mystery writer Stephen King had been heard to comment that the style of novels he was best known for had as much literary worth as those of the renowned giants of fiction. As this graphic shows, he is only six degrees of separation from some of the greatest writers ever.

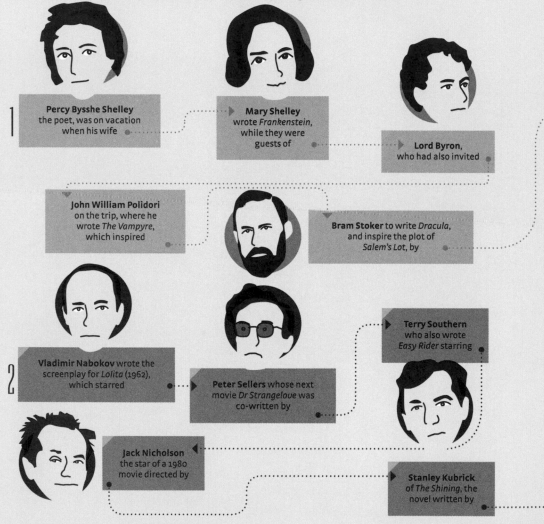

1

Percy Bysshe Shelley
the poet, was on vacation when his wife

Mary Shelley
wrote *Frankenstein*, while they were guests of

Lord Byron,
who had also invited

John William Polidori
on the trip, where he wrote *The Vampyre*, which inspired

Bram Stoker to write *Dracula*, and inspire the plot of *Salem's Lot*, by

2

Vladimir Nabokov wrote the screenplay for *Lolita* (1962), which starred

Peter Sellers whose next movie *Dr Strangelove* was co-written by

Terry Southern
who also wrote *Easy Rider* starring

Jack Nicholson
the star of a 1980 movie directed by

Stanley Kubrick
of *The Shining*, the novel written by

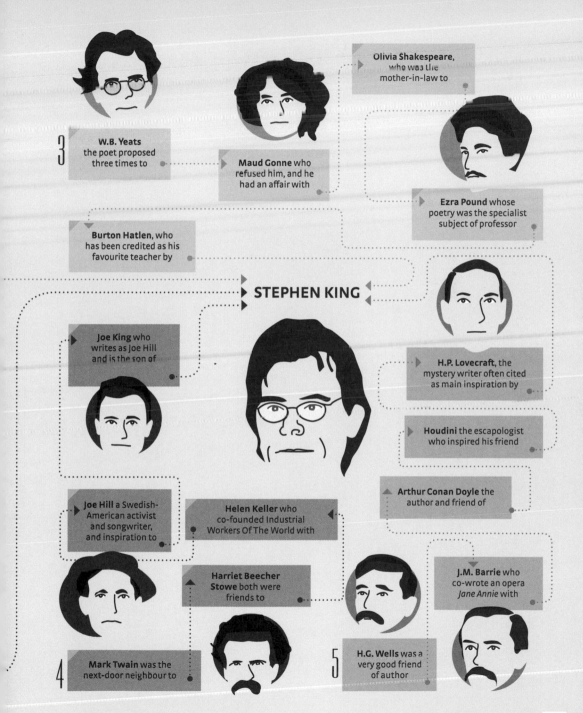

Olivia Shakespeare, who was the mother-in-law to

3 **W.B. Yeats** the poet proposed three times to

Maud Gonne who refused him, and he had an affair with

Ezra Pound whose poetry was the specialist subject of professor

Burton Hatlen, who has been credited as his favourite teacher by

STEPHEN KING

Joe King who writes as Joe Hill and is the son of

H.P. Lovecraft, the mystery writer often cited as main inspiration by

Houdini the escapologist who inspired his friend

Joe Hill a Swedish-American activist and songwriter, and inspiration to

Helen Keller who co-founded Industrial Workers Of The World with

Arthur Conan Doyle the author and friend of

J.M. Barrie who co-wrote an opera *Jane Annie* with

Harriet Beecher Stowe both were friends to

4 **Mark Twain** was the next-door neighbour to

5 **H.G. Wells** was a very good friend of author

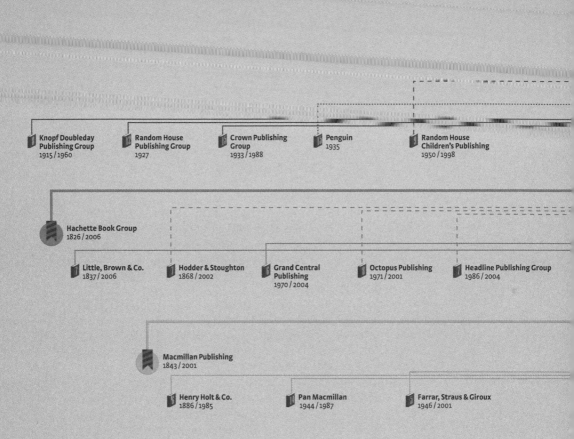

Knopf Doubleday Publishing Group
1915 / 1960

Random House Publishing Group
1927

Crown Publishing Group
1933 / 1988

Penguin
1935

Random House Children's Publishing
1950 / 1998

Hachette Book Group
1826 / 2006

Little, Brown & Co.
1837 / 2006

Hodder & Stoughton
1868 / 2002

Grand Central Publishing
1970 / 2004

Octopus Publishing
1971 / 2001

Headline Publishing Group
1986 / 2004

Macmillan Publishing
1843 / 2001

Henry Holt & Co.
1886 / 1985

Pan Macmillan
1944 / 1987

Farrar, Straus & Giroux
1946 / 2001

A BRIEF HISTORY OF THE BIG FIVE
PUBLISHING COMPANIES

The world's major publishing companies are run by five separate and different media conglomerates. Here's who they are, which publishing houses they own and how many different imprints each has.

Parent group
Country, year formed

Publishing house
Year formed, year acquired

Publishing group
Year formed, year acquired, and total imprints

Imprint
Year formed, year acquired

Harper
1817

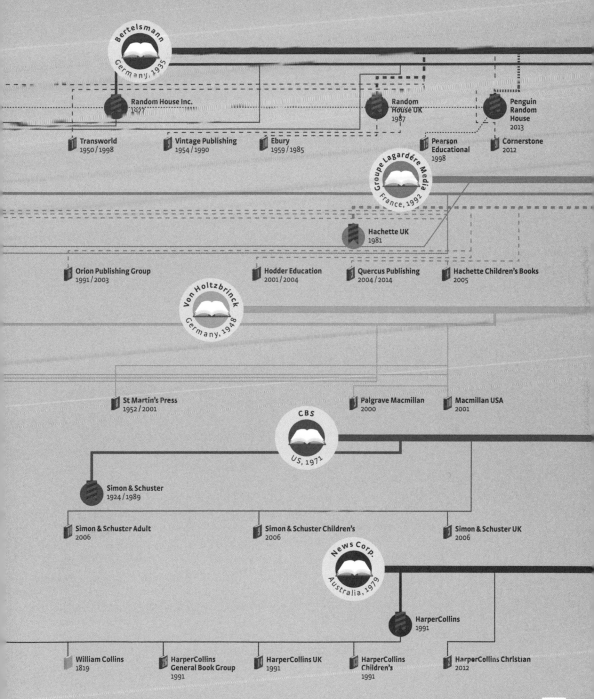

Bertelsmann
Germany, 1935

Random House Inc.
1927

Random House UK
1987

Penguin Random House
2013

Transworld
1950 / 1998

Vintage Publishing
1954 / 1990

Ebury
1959 / 1985

Pearson Educational
1998

Cornerstone
2012

Groupe Lagardére Media
France, 1992

Hachette UK
1981

Orion Publishing Group
1991 / 2003

Hodder Education
2001 / 2004

Quercus Publishing
2004 / 2014

Hachette Children's Books
2005

Von Holtzbrinck
Germany, 1948

St Martin's Press
1952 / 2001

Palgrave Macmillan
2000

Macmillan USA
2001

CBS
US, 1971

Simon & Schuster
1924 / 1989

Simon & Schuster Adult
2006

Simon & Schuster Children's
2006

Simon & Schuster UK
2006

News Corp.
Australia, 1979

HarperCollins
1991

William Collins
1819

HarperCollins General Book Group
1991

HarperCollins UK
1991

HarperCollins Children's
1991

HarperCollins Christian
2012

1781

CRITIQUE OF PURE REASON

Immanuel Kant

ONTOLOGY

The nature of being

1869

CULTURE AND ANARCHY

Mathew Arnold

LITERARY CRITICISM

Methodology of the study of literature

1899

THE INTERPRETATION OF DREAMS

Sigmund Freud

PSYCHOANALYSIS

Human mental development

1914

INTRODUCTION TO THE STUDY OF LANGUAGE

Leonard Bloomfield

STRUCTURAL LINGUISTICS

Syntagmatic and paradigmatic analysis

1936

THE WORK OF ART IN THE AGE OF MECHANICAL REPRODUCTION

Walter Benjamin

PHILOSOPHY OF TECHNOLOGY

The nature of technology and social effects

1956

FUNDAMENTALS OF LANGUAGE

Roman Jakobson

STRUCTURALISM

Structural analysis of language

1963

CULTURE AND SOCIETY

Raymond Williams

MARXIST

Interpreting texts through Marxist theory

1967

DEATH OF THE AUTHOR

Roland Barthes

POST-STRUCTURALISM

Mediation between concrete reality and abstraction

1977

THE MODES OF MODERN WRITING

David Lodge

LITERARY THEORY

The nature of literature

1978

THE ACT OF READING: A THEORY OF AESTHETIC RESPONSE

Wolfgang Iser

RECEPTION THEORY

Reader response to text

1990

GENDER TROUBLE: FEMINISM AND THE SUBVERSION OF IDENTITY

Judith Butler

FEMINIST THEORY

Feminist-based reading of texts

1990

EPISTEMOLOGY OF THE CLOSET

Eve Kosofsky Sedgwick

QUEER THEORY

Post-structuralist reading of queer interpretations of text

1916	1927	1928	1928
COURS DE LINGUISTIQUE GÉNÉRALE Ferdinand de Saussure 👓 SEMIOTICS	**BEING AND TIME** Martin Heidegger ☿ EXISTENTIAL PHENOMENOLOGY	**THE PRINCIPLES OF LITERARY CRITICISM** I.A. Richards 👓 NEW CRITICISM	**ON THE PHENOMENOLOGY OF THE CONSCIOUSNESS OF INTERNAL TIME** Edmund Husserl ☿ PHENOMENOLOGY
Signs, signifiers and the signified	*Being*	*Close reading of texts (sustained interpretation of brief passages)*	*Experience and consciousness*

1967	1967	1975	1976–1984
VALIDITY IN INTERPRETATION E.D. Hirsch Jr. 👓 HERMENEUTICS	**OF GRAMMATOLOGY** Jacques Derrida 👓 DECONSTRUCTION	**THE DIALOGIC IMAGINATION** Mikhail Bakhtin ☿ PHILOSOPHY OF LANGUAGE	**THE HISTORY OF SEXUALITY** Michel Foucault 👓 POST-MODERNISM
Interpreting text by historical retrieval of context	*Metaphysics of presence*	*The nature of meaning, language use, cognition, language and reality*	*Elusive definition of text, non-conformist principles of structure*

EVERYONE'S A **CRITIC**

With open access on bookselling websites for people to 'review' a title, everyone can be a critic. Very few of us, however, have been trained to do it. In case you're thinking of getting serious about literary criticism, this handy guide to the main schools of criticism, their leading critics and the major philosophical schools that inform much of the theory, provide a handy study list.

👓 Theory ☿ Philosophy

● Switzerland ● Germany ● Wales ● France ● USA ● England ● Russia

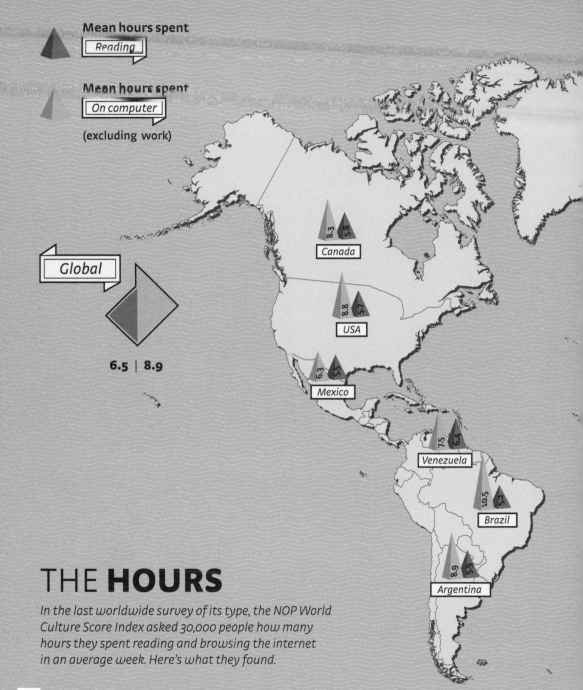

Mean hours spent
Reading

Mean hours spent
On computer
(excluding work)

Global

6.5 | 8.9

8.3 5.8 _Canada_

8.8 5.7 _USA_

6.3 5.5 _Mexico_

7.5 6.4 _Venezuela_

10.5 5.2 _Brazil_

8.9 5.9 _Argentina_

THE **HOURS**

In the last worldwide survey of its type, the NOP World
Culture Score Index asked 30,000 people how many
hours they spent reading and browsing the internet
in an average week. Here's what they found.

THE **THRILLER** STARTER KIT

Of all the genres favoured by self-published authors, the thriller is most popular. But how to get started? Here is a formula to find a title, names of the main characters and even the self-publishing imprint. The rest is up to your imagination.

Your book title

☐ + ☐ + ☐

Your main protagonist's first name and occupation

☐ + ☐

Your main villain's first name and occupation

☐ + ☐

Your self-publishing imprint name

☐ + ☐ + ☐

SELECT MONTH OF YOUR BIRTH DATE Title link (if needed)
SELECT CURRENT MONTH Protagonist's first name
SELECT MONTH OF YOUR BIRTH DATE Villain's first name

SELECT MONTH OF YOUR BIRTH DATE Imprint first word
SELECT CURRENT MONTH Imprint second word
SELECT MONTH OF PUBLICATION Imprint third word

JANUARY
- In
- **M** Adam **or F** Eve
- **M** no name **or F** Helen
- Black
- Tarantula
- Books

FEBRUARY
- To
- **M** Jack **or F** Jill
- **M** Butler **or F** Annie
- Red
- Lizard
- Press

MARCH
- If
- **M** Kurt **or F** Saga
- **M** King **or F** Alex
- Green
- Panther
- Publishing

APRIL
- The
- **M** Mike **or F** Betty
- **M** Self **or F** Medea
- Blue
- Crow
- Mysteries

MAY
- Not
- **M** Ford **or F** Berlin
- **M** Smith **or F** Lee
- Violet
- Vulture
- Stories

JUNE
- So
- **M** Harry **or F** Cassandra
- **M** Riuchi **or F** Glenn
- Crimson
- Marmoset
- Library

JULY
- Of
- **M** Chance **or F** Cordelia
- **M** Henry **or F** Nurse 'x'
- Purple
- Swan
- Collection

AUGUST
- From
- **M** Simeon **or F** Antigone
- **M** Price **or F** Mrs X
- Orange
- Shark
- Corps.

SEPTEMBER
- And
- **M** Hermes **or F** P.D.
- **M** Daddy **or F** Mamma
- Grey
- Mosquito
- House

OCTOBER
- But
- **M** Josef **or F** Lissy
- **M** Kurt **or F** Cruella
- Pink
- Arachnid
- Series

NOVEMBER
- Have
- **M** Siggi **or F** Frankie
- **M** H **or F** E
- Lime
- Wolf
- & Co.

DECEMBER
- As
- **M** Ulysses **or F** Molly
- **M** Yussuf **or F** Betty
- White
- Dog
- Brothers

SUNDAY	MONDAY	TUESDAY	WEDNESDAY	THURSDAY	FRIDAY	SATURDAY
SELECT YOUR BIRTH DATE — Single title or first word			**1** — Caught / Sleep / Police / Police	**2** — Return / Blood / Lawyer / Organized crime employee	**3** — Fatal / Rain / Coroner / Psychopath or sociopath	**4** — Forget / Time / Private detective / Cyber criminal
SELECT TODAY'S DATE — Predicative adjective for the title						
DAY OF THE WEEK (TODAY'S DATE) — Protagonist's occupation						
DAY OF THE WEEK (YOUR BIRTH DATE) — Villain's occupation						
5 — Memory / Home / Armed forces (or ex-) / PTS sufferer	**6** — Echo / Forlorn / Ex-elite military or federal police / Ex-lover	**7** — Outside / Run / Average civilian / Celebrity with a secret	**8** — Cry / Hell / Police / Police	**9** — Gone / Past / Lawyer / Organized crime employee	**10** — Still / Them / Coroner / Psychopath or sociopath	**11** — Cold / Away / Private detective / Cyber criminal
12 — Found / Forgotten / Armed forces (or ex-) / PTS sufferer	**13** — Child / Rules / Ex-elite military or federal police / Ex-lover	**14** — Storm / Place / Average civilian / Celebrity with a secret	**15** — Fall / Money / Police / Police	**16** — Just / Grave / Lawyer / Organized crime employee	**17** — Boy / Eyes / Coroner / Psychopath or sociopath	**18** — Long / Chance / Private detective / Cyber criminal
19 — Little / Nothing / Armed forces (or ex-) / PTS sufferer	**20** — Final / Beloved / Ex-elite military or federal police / Ex-lover	**21** — Naked / Hole / Average civilian / Celebrity with a secret	**22** — Girl / Disappeared / Police / Police	**23** — Fear / When / Lawyer / Organized crime employee	**24** — Believe / Heaven / Coroner / Psychopath or sociopath	**25** — Back / Here / Private detective / Cyber criminal
26 — Blind / Them / Armed forces (or ex-) / PTS sufferer	**27** — Missing / Ending / Ex-elite military or federal police / Ex-lover	**28** — Shame / Song / Average civilian / Celebrity with a secret	**29** — Watch / Forever / Police / Police	**30** — Losing / Time / Lawyer / Organized crime employee	**31** — Thirteen / Again / Coroner / Psychopath or sociopath	THE END

135

BIG SCREEN **WRITERS**

★ REAL AUTHOR ★

box office ▶	$1m ▶	$1.65m ▶	$2.2m ▶
REAL AUTHOR MOVIE & YEAR	**T.S. Eliot** (1888–1965, USA) *Tom And Viv* *(1994)*	**Joe Orton** (1933–1967, England) *Prick Up Your Ears* *(1987)*	**Oscar Wilde** (1854–1900, Ireland) *Wilde* *(1998)*

$2.9m ▶	$4.2m ▶	$6.1m ▶	$10.9m ▶
Sylvia Plath (1932– 1963, USA), **Ted Hughes** (1930–1998, England) *Sylvia (2003)*	**Dorothy Parker** (1893–1967, USA) *Mrs Parker And The Vicious Circle* *(1994)*	**Knut Hamsun** (1859–1952, Norway) *Hamsun* *(1996)*	**Jean-Baptiste Poquelin (AKA Molière)** (1622–1673, France) *Molière* *(2007)*

$14.4m ▶	$16.15m ▶	$23.5m ▶	$35m ▶
John Keats (1795–1821, England) *Bright Star* *(2009)*	**Iris Murdoch** (1919–1999, Ireland) *Iris* *(2001)*	**Henry Miller** (1891–1980, USA), **Anaïs Nin** (1903–1977, France) *Henry & June (1990)*	**Beatrix Potter** (1866–1943, England) *Miss Potter* *(2006)*

$49.2m ▶	$109m ▶	$112.5m ▶	$289.3m ▶
Truman Capote (1924–1984, USA) *Capote* *(2005)*	**Virginia Woolf** (1882–1941, England) *The Hours* *(2002)*	**P.L. Travers** (1899–1996, Australia) *Saving Mr Banks* *(2013)*	**William Shakespeare** (1582–1616, England) *Shakespeare In Love* *(1998)*

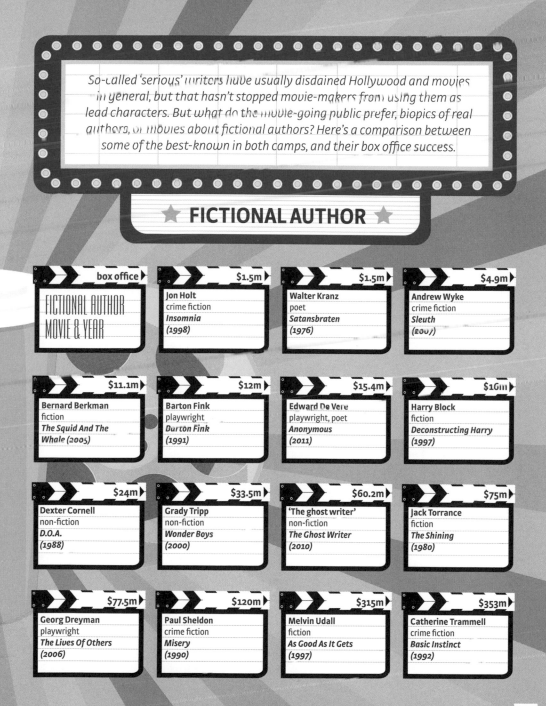

So-called 'serious' writers have usually disdained Hollywood and movies in general, but that hasn't stopped movie-makers from using them as lead characters. But what do the movie-going public prefer, biopics of real authors, or movies about fictional authors? Here's a comparison between some of the best-known in both camps, and their box office success.

★ FICTIONAL AUTHOR ★

box office ▶

FICTIONAL AUTHOR MOVIE & YEAR

$1.5m ▶

Jon Holt
crime fiction
Insomnia
(1998)

$1.5m ▶

Walter Kranz
poet
Satansbraten
(1976)

$4.9m ▶

Andrew Wyke
crime fiction
Sleuth
(2007)

$11.1m ▶

Bernard Berkman
fiction
The Squid And The Whale (2005)

$12m ▶

Barton Fink
playwright
Barton Fink
(1991)

$15.4m ▶

Edward De Vere
playwright, poet
Anonymous
(2011)

$16m ▶

Harry Block
fiction
Deconstructing Harry
(1997)

$24m ▶

Dexter Cornell
non-fiction
D.O.A.
(1988)

$33.5m ▶

Grady Tripp
non-fiction
Wonder Boys
(2000)

$60.2m ▶

'The ghost writer'
non-fiction
The Ghost Writer
(2010)

$75m ▶

Jack Torrance
fiction
The Shining
(1980)

$77.5m ▶

Georg Dreyman
playwright
The Lives Of Others
(2006)

$120m ▶

Paul Sheldon
crime fiction
Misery
(1990)

$315m ▶

Melvin Udall
fiction
As Good As It Gets
(1997)

$353m ▶

Catherine Trammell
crime fiction
Basic Instinct
(1992)

BEAT HAPPENINGS

With the opening of the City Lights book store in San Francisco, the Beat Generation had a base from which to conquer the world with their jazz-inflected poetry and prose. Here are the main Beat happenings, the Beats and their key works.

City Lights – bookstore opening, 1953
261 Columbus Avenue,
San Francisco, CA, USA

- ● *City Lights* magazine, 1952
- △ ● *A Coney Island Of The Mind*, 1958
- ● Manager City Lights Pocket Bookstore, 1953–1976
- ● Editor City Lights magazine and books, executive director, 1971–2007

Howl obscenity trial, 1957
Municipal Court,
San Francisco, CA, USA

Reading at the Six Gallery, 1955
261 Columbus Avenue,
San Francisco, CA, USA

- ● Artist and co-owner of Six Gallery, 1954–1965
- △ ● *Ekstasis*, 1959
- △ ● *On Bear's Head*, 1960
- △ ● *Turtle Island*, 1974
- △ ● *The New Book/A Book Of Torture*, 1961
- △ ● *Howl*, 1955

- ● Peter D. Martin (1923–)
- ● Lawrence Ferlinghetti (1919–)
- ● Shig Murao (1926–1999)
- ● Nancy Joyce Peters (1936–)
- ● Wally Hendrick (1928–2003)
- ● Philip Lamantia (1927–2005)
- ● Philip Whalen (1923–2002)
- ● Gary Snyder (1934–)
- ● Michael McLure (1932–)
- ● Allen Ginsberg (1927–1997)
- ● Judge Clayton W. Horn (1904–1981)
- ● Gilbert Millstein (1915–1999)
- ● Jack Kerouac (1922–1969)

- ● Neal Cassady (1926–1968)
- ● Peter Orlovsky (1933–2010)
- ● William S. Burroughs (1914–1997)
- ● Gregory Corso (1930–2001)
- ● Harold Norse (1916–2009)
- ● Brion Gysin (1916–1986, UK)
- ● Ian Sommerville (1940–1976, UK)
- ● Adrian Mitchell (1932–2008, UK)
- ● Alexander Trocchi (1925–1984, UK)
- ● Anselm Hollo (1934–2013, Fin)
- ● Michael Horovitz (1935–, UK)
- ● Simon Vinkenoog (1928–2009, Ned)

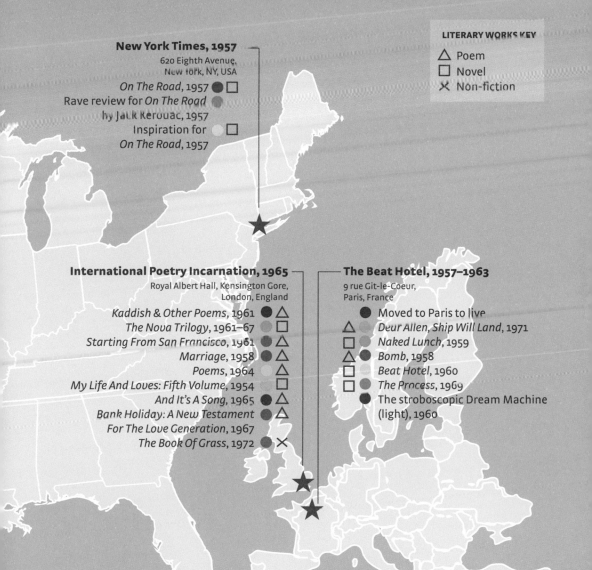

LITERARY WORKS KEY

△ Poem
□ Novel
✕ Non-fiction

New York Times, 1957

620 Eighth Avenue,
New York, NY, USA

On The Road, 1957 ● □
Rave review for On The Road ●
by Jack Kerouac, 1957
Inspiration for ● □
On The Road, 1957

International Poetry Incarnation, 1965

Royal Albert Hall, Kensington Gore,
London, England

Kaddish & Other Poems, 1961 ● △
The Nova Trilogy, 1961–67 ● □
Starting From San Francisco, 1961 ● △
Marriage, 1958 ● △
Poems, 1964 ● △
My Life And Loves: Fifth Volume, 1954 ● □
And It's A Song, 1965 ● △
Bank Holiday: A New Testament ● △
For The Love Generation, 1967
The Book Of Grass, 1972 ● ✕

The Beat Hotel, 1957–1963

9 rue Git-le-Coeur,
Paris, France

● Moved to Paris to live
△ Dear Allen, Ship Will Land, 1971
□ Naked Lunch, 1959
△ Bomb, 1958
□ Beat Hotel, 1960
□ The Process, 1969
● The stroboscopic Dream Machine
(light), 1960

BOYS WILL BE **GIRLS**

*Sometimes it's hard to be a woman. Or a man. Authors who have chosen
to write under a pseudonym of the opposite gender have done so for a
variety of reasons, but is there one rule for boys and another for girls?*

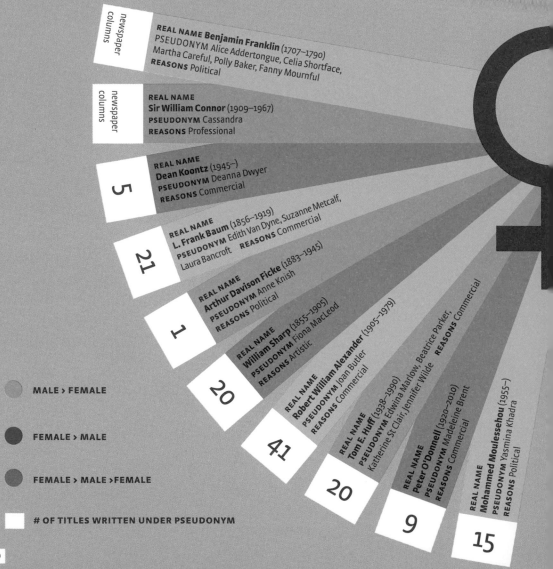

newspaper columns

REAL NAME Benjamin Franklin (1707–1790)
PSEUDONYM Alice Addertongue, Celia Shortface,
Martha Careful, Polly Baker, Fanny Mournful
REASONS Political

newspaper columns

REAL NAME
Sir William Connor (1909–1967)
PSEUDONYM Cassandra
REASONS Professional

5

REAL NAME
Dean Koontz (1945–)
PSEUDONYM Deanna Dwyer
REASONS Commercial

21

REAL NAME
L. Frank Baum (1856–1919)
PSEUDONYM Edith Van Dyne, Suzanne Metcalf,
Laura Bancroft   **REASONS** Commercial

1

REAL NAME
Arthur Davison Ficke (1883–1945)
PSEUDONYM Anne Knish
REASONS Political

20

REAL NAME
William Sharp (1855–1905)
PSEUDONYM Fiona MacLeod
REASONS Artistic

41

REAL NAME
Robert William Alexander (1905–1979)
PSEUDONYM Joan Butler
REASONS Commercial

20

REAL NAME
Tom E. Huff (1938–1990)
PSEUDONYM Edwina Marlow, Beatrice Parker,
Katherine St Clair, Jennifer Wilde   **REASONS** Commercial

9

REAL NAME
Peter O'Donnell (1920–2010)
PSEUDONYM Madeleine Brent
REASONS Commercial

15

REAL NAME
Mohammed Moulessehou (1955–)
PSEUDONYM Yasmina Khadra
REASONS Political

- MALE > FEMALE
- FEMALE > MALE
- FEMALE > MALE >FEMALE

 # OF TITLES WRITTEN UNDER PSEUDONYM

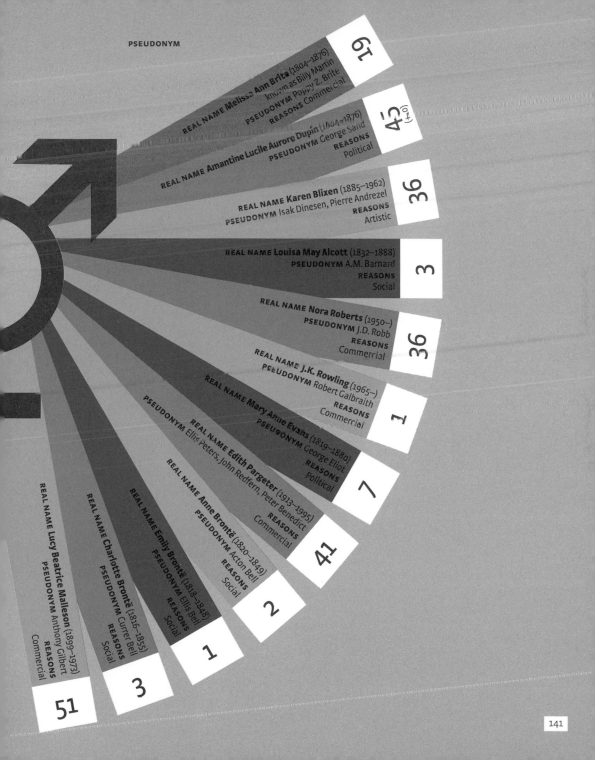

19

REAL NAME **Melissa Ann Brite** (1904–1976)
known as Billy Martin
PSEUDONYM Poppy Z. Brite
REASONS Commercial

45 (+0)

REAL NAME **Amantine Lucile Aurore Dupin** (1804–1876)
PSEUDONYM George Sand
REASONS Political

36

REAL NAME **Karen Blixen** (1885–1962)
PSEUDONYM Isak Dinesen, Pierre Andrezel
REASONS Artistic

3

REAL NAME **Louisa May Alcott** (1832–1888)
PSEUDONYM A.M. Barnard
REASONS Social

36

REAL NAME **Nora Roberts** (1950–)
PSEUDONYM J.D. Robb
REASONS Commercial

1

REAL NAME **J.K. Rowling** (1965–)
PSEUDONYM Robert Galbraith
REASONS Commercial

7

REAL NAME **Mary Anne Evans** (1819–1880)
PSEUDONYM George Eliot
REASONS Political

41

REAL NAME **Edith Pargeter** (1913–1995)
PSEUDONYM Ellis Peters, John Redfern, Peter Benedict
REASONS Commercial

2

REAL NAME **Anne Brontë** (1820–1849)
PSEUDONYM Acton Bell
REASONS Social

1

REAL NAME **Emily Brontë** (1818–1848)
PSEUDONYM Ellis Bell
REASONS Social

3

REAL NAME **Charlotte Brontë** (1816–1855)
PSEUDONYM Currer Bell
REASONS Social

51

REAL NAME **Lucy Beatrice Malleson** (1899–1973)
PSEUDONYM Anthony Gilbert
REASONS Commercial

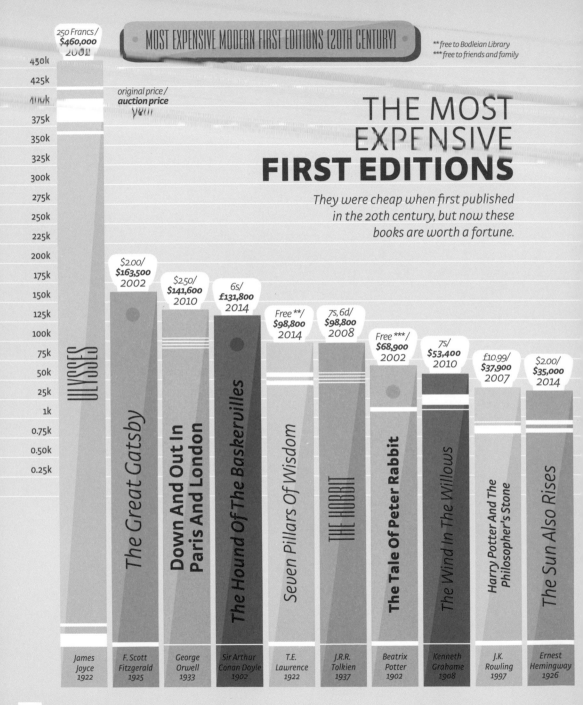

** free to Bodleian Library
*** free to friends and family

THE MOST
EXPENSIVE
FIRST EDITIONS

They were cheap when first published
in the 20th century, but now these
books are worth a fortune.

450k
425k
400k
375k
350k
325k
300k
275k
250k
225k
200k
175k
150k
125k
100k
75k
50k
25k
1k
0.75k
0.50k
0.25k

original price /
auction price
year

250 Francs /
$460,000
2002

$2.00/
$163,500
2002

$2.50/
$141,600
2010

6s/
£131,800
2014

Free **/
$98,800
2014

7s, 6d/
$98,800
2008

Free *** /
$68,900
2002

7s/
$53,400
2010

£10.99/
$37,900
2007

$2.00/
$35,000
2014

ULYSSES

The Great Gatsby

Down And Out In
Paris And London

The Hound Of The Baskervilles

Seven Pillars Of Wisdom

THE HOBBIT

The Tale Of Peter Rabbit

The Wind In The Willows

Harry Potter And The
Philosopher's Stone

The Sun Also Rises

James
Joyce
1922

F. Scott
Fitzgerald
1925

George
Orwell
1933

Sir Arthur
Conan Doyle
1902

T.E.
Lawrence
1922

J.R.R.
Tolkien
1937

Beatrix
Potter
1902

Kenneth
Grahame
1908

J.K.
Rowling
1997

Ernest
Hemingway
1926

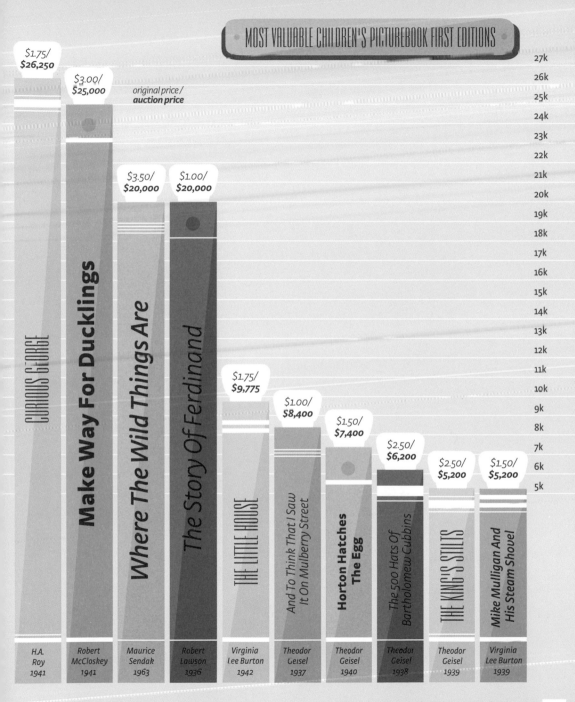

$1.75/$26,250

CURIOUS GEORGE

H.A. Roy 1941

$3.00/$25,000

original price/ **auction price**

Make Way For Ducklings

Robert McCloskey 1941

$3.50/$20,000

Where The Wild Things Are

Maurice Sendak 1963

$1.00/$20,000

The Story Of Ferdinand

Robert Lawson 1936

$1.75/$9,775

THE LITTLE HOUSE

Virginia Lee Burton 1942

$1.00/$8,400

And To Think That I Saw It On Mulberry Street

Theodor Geisel 1937

$1.50/$7,400

Horton Hatches The Egg

Theodor Geisel 1940

$2.50/$6,200

The 500 Hats Of Bartholomew Cubbins

Theodor Geisel 1938

$2.50/$5,200

THE KING'S STILTS

Theodor Geisel 1939

$1.50/$5,200

Mike Mulligan And His Steam Shovel

Virginia Lee Burton 1939

27k
26k
25k
24k
23k
22k
21k
20k
19k
18k
17k
16k
15k
14k
13k
12k
11k
10k
9k
8k
7k
6k
5k

Henry James

1843 USA
1916 England

England 1876 / Personal

14*

(A)

Portrait Of A Lady (1880)

Thomas Mann

1875 Germany
1955 Switzerland

Switzerland 1933 / Political
USA 1939 / Political
Switzerland 1952 / Personal

5

(C)

Lotte In Weimar:
The Beloved Returns (1939)

James Joyce

1882 Ireland
1941 Switzerland

Austria-Hungary 1904 / Professional
Switzerland 1915 / Professional
France 1920 / Personal
Zurich 1940 / Political

5

(N)

Ulysses (1922)

Vladimir Nabokov

1899 Russia
1977 Switzerland

Ukraine 1917 / Political
England 1919 / Political
Germany 1922 / Professional
France 1937 / Political
USA 1940 / Political
Switzerland 1961 / Personal

18*

(N)

Ada Or Ardor:
A Family Chronicle (1969)

V.S. Naipaul

1932 Trinidad
–

England 1950 / Educational

14

(N)

A Bend In The River (1979)

Salman Rushdie

1947 India

England 1958 / Educational
USA 2000 / Commercial

14*

(?)

The Satanic Verses (1988)

EXILE'S **KINGDOM**

*Literature is peppered with authors who have found an
audience by writing about their homeland from which they
are exiled. Here are arguably the dozen most famous writers
in exile, where they moved to, why, and their key novel.*

Mohsin Hamid

1971 **Pakistan**

—

USA 1974–1980 / Personal
USA 1989–2001 / Educational
England 2001–2009
/ Professional

3

Ⓐ

The Reluctant
Fundamentalist (2007)

Chimamanda Ngozi Adichie

1977 **Nigeria**

—

USA 1996 / Educational

2*

Ⓐ

Half Of A Yellow Sun (2006)

Marjane Satrapi

1969 **Iran**

—

Austria 1983–1988 / Political,
Educational
France 1994 / Political

11

Ⓒ

Persepolis (2000)

Rohinton Mistry

1952 **India**

—

Canada 1975 / Educational

6

Ⓒ

Such A Long Journey (1991)

Kiran Desai

1972 **India**

—

England 1985 / Personal
USA 1986 / Educational

2

Ⓝ

The Inheritance Of Loss (2006)

Junot Diaz

1968 **Dominican Republic**

—

USA 1974 / Personal

2*

Ⓝ

The Brief Wondrous Life
Of Oscar Wao (2007)

Author
b. country
d. country
emigrated to, when / reason for move
works published in exile
Ⓒ critical / Ⓝ nostalgic / Ⓐ ambiguous about homeland
key work

(* novels only)

LOSE THE NAME OF **ACTION**

Shakespeare's Hamlet *has inspired so many literary works, including poetry, plays, movies, songs, novels and criticism, that it is arguably the most inspirational work of literature ever. Here we discover that Act III – and the 'To be or not to be' soliloquy in particular – is by far the most quoted.*

Year	Author	Work
1875	Bram Stoker	*Dracula*
1922	Edith Wharton	*The Glimpses Of The Moon*
1922	Aldous Huxley	*Mortal Coils*
1921	David Lloyd George	*Slings And Arrows*
1930	Graham Greene	*The Name Of Action*
1933	John Masefield	*Bird Of Dawning*
1935	Ogden Nash	*The Primrose Path*
1939	Georgette Heyer	*No Wind Of Blame*
1947	Louis Auchincloss	*The Indifferent Children*
1948	Clifford Bax	*Rosemary For Remembrance*
1952	Agatha Christie	*The Mousetrap*
1955	Monica Dickens	*The Winds Of Heaven*
1959	Philip K. Dick	*Time Out Of Joint*
1966	Tom Stoppard	*Rosencrantz And Guildenstern Are Dead*
1967	Nigel Balchin	*Kings Of Infinite Space*
1969	Marguerite Duras	*A Sea Of Troubles*
1969	Richard Yates	*A Special Providence*
1971	D.H. Lawrence	*The Mortal Coil And Other Stories*
1972	Isaac Asimov	*The Gods Themselves*
1978	Richard Matheson	*What Dreams May Come*
1980	Anthony Powell	*Infants Of The Spring*
1987	Lee Strasberg	*A Dream Of Passion: The Development Of The Method*
1991	Robert B. Parker	*Perchance To Dream*
1996	David Foster Wallace	*Infinite Jest*
2004	Jasper Fforde	*Something Rotten*

[of which 'To Be Or Not To Be' soliloquy 8%]

ACT I	ACT II	ACT III	ACT IV	ACT V
24.5%	15.5%	39%	8%	10%

ALL THE **DEAD** YOUR POETS

ALL THE **DEAD**
YOUNG POETS

When Keats died of TB in 1821 aged 25, and Shelley drowned the following year aged 29, it seemed to begin a sad tradition of fiery young poets who lived and loved too much, dying before reaching the age of 40. Here are the greatest since then to have left this earth before their time.*

CAUSE OF DEATH

Tuberculosis
Drowning
Suicide
Other

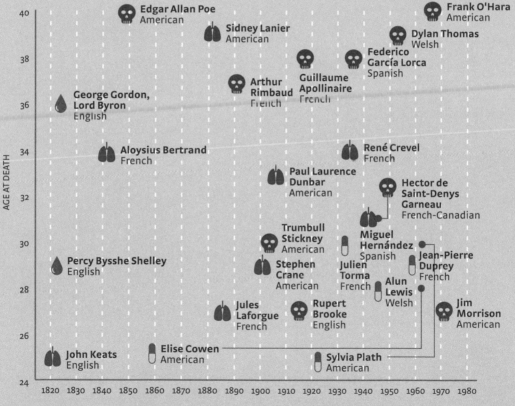

AGE AT DEATH

40

Edgar Allan Poe
American

Frank O'Hara
American

Sidney Lanier
American

Dylan Thomas
Welsh

38

Federico
García Lorca
Spanish

Guillaume
Apollinaire
French

Arthur
Rimbaud
French

George Gordon,
Lord Byron
English

36

Aloysius Bertrand
French

34

René Crevel
French

Paul Laurence
Dunbar
American

Hector de
Saint-Denys
Garneau
French-Canadian

32

Trumbull
Stickney
American

Miguel
Hernández
Spanish

Jean-Pierre
Duprey
French

30

Percy Bysshe Shelley
English

Stephen
Crane
American

Julien
Torma
French

Alun
Lewis
Welsh

28

Jules
Laforgue
French

Rupert
Brooke
English

Jim
Morrison
American

26

Elise Cowen
American

Sylvia Plath
American

John Keats
English

24

1820 1830 1840 1850 1860 1870 1880 1890 1900 1910 1920 1930 1940 1950 1960 1970 1980

YEAR

* not including those killed in action during wars

DEAR **READER**

You, dear reader, can feel incredibly close to the characters on the page, and perhaps even closer to the person who put them there: the author. As this graphic shows, the dear reader is never more than six degrees away from the writer.

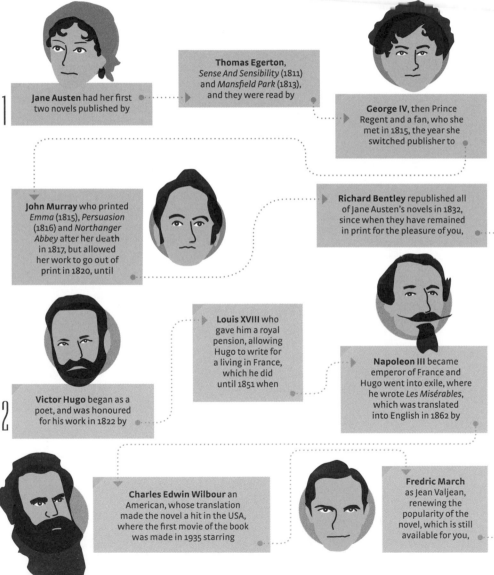

1

Jane Austen had her first two novels published by

Thomas Egerton, *Sense And Sensibility* (1811) and *Mansfield Park* (1813), and they were read by

George IV, then Prince Regent and a fan, who she met in 1815, the year she switched publisher to

John Murray who printed *Emma* (1815), *Persuasion* (1816) and *Northanger Abbey* after her death in 1817, but allowed her work to go out of print in 1820, until

Richard Bentley republished all of Jane Austen's novels in 1832, since when they have remained in print for the pleasure of you,

Louis XVIII who gave him a royal pension, allowing Hugo to write for a living in France, which he did until 1851 when

2

Victor Hugo began as a poet, and was honoured for his work in 1822 by

Napoleon III became emperor of France and Hugo went into exile, where he wrote *Les Misérables*, which was translated into English in 1862 by

Charles Edwin Wilbour an American, whose translation made the novel a hit in the USA, where the first movie of the book was made in 1935 starring

Fredric March as Jean Valjean, renewing the popularity of the novel, which is still available for you,

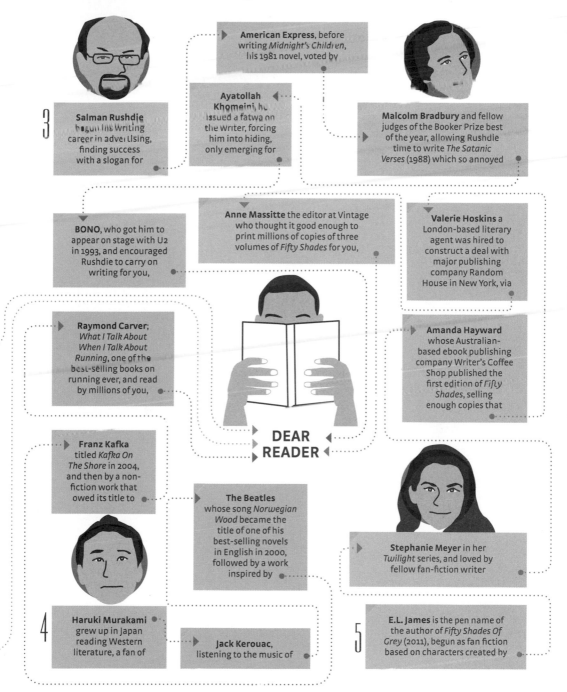

3

Salman Rushdie began his writing career in advertising, finding success with a slogan for

American Express, before writing *Midnight's Children*, his 1981 novel, voted by

Ayatollah Khomeini, he issued a fatwa on the writer, forcing him into hiding, only emerging for

Malcolm Bradbury and fellow judges of the Booker Prize best of the year, allowing Rushdie time to write *The Satanic Verses* (1988) which so annoyed

BONO, who got him to appear on stage with U2 in 1993, and encouraged Rushdie to carry on writing for you,

Anne Massitte the editor at Vintage who thought it good enough to print millions of copies of three volumes of *Fifty Shades* for you,

Valerie Hoskins a London-based literary agent was hired to construct a deal with major publishing company Random House in New York, via

Raymond Carver; *What I Talk About When I Talk About Running*, one of the best-selling books on running ever, and read by millions of you,

DEAR READER

Amanda Hayward whose Australian-based ebook publishing company Writer's Coffee Shop published the first edition of *Fifty Shades*, selling enough copies that

Franz Kafka titled *Kafka On The Shore* in 2004, and then by a non-fiction work that owed its title to

The Beatles whose song *Norwegian Wood* became the title of one of his best-selling novels in English in 2000, followed by a work inspired by

Stephanie Meyer in her *Twilight* series, and loved by fellow fan-fiction writer

4

Haruki Murakami grew up in Japan reading Western literature, a fan of

Jack Kerouac, listening to the music of

5

E.L. James is the pen name of the author of *Fifty Shades Of Grey* (2011), begun as fan fiction based on characters created by

WHAT'S THE **WEATHER** LIKE?

*From Homer to James Herbert via Shakespeare and Victor Hugo,
the weather in fiction has played an important part in underpinning
a sense of mood, pointing up intention and acting as a metaphor.
Here are 40 uses of different types of
weather in classics of literature
and what they represent.*

STORMS

King Lear William Shakespeare (1603–1607)

MADNESS *Wuthering Heights* Emily Brontë (1845–46)

EMOTIONAL TURMOIL *Lord Of The Flies* William Golding (1954) VIOLENCE *The Odyssey*

Homer (BC8) TURMOIL *Jude The Obscure* Thomas Hardy (1895) DEATH

Great Expectations Charles Dickens (1861) MALEVOLENT WORLD *The Seagull* Anton Chekhov

(1895) CHANGE *Les Misérables* Victor Hugo (1862) DEFEAT *One Day In The Life Of Ivan*

Denisovich Aleksandr Solzhenitsyn (1962) MALEVOLENT WORLD *Lord Jim* Joseph

Conrad (1900) DISORDER *The Aenid* Virgil (BC19–29) RAGE

SNOW

A Farewell To Arms Ernest Hemingway

(1929) HOPE *The Lion, The Witch And The Wardrobe* C.S. Lewis

(1950) LOSS OF HOPE *Ethan Frome* Edith Wharton (1911) ISOLATION *The*

Dead James Joyce (1914) DESOLATION *A Child's Christmas In Wales* Dylan Thomas

(1955) NOSTALGIA *Andorra* Max Frisch (1961) HIDDEN CRIMES

SUN

Walden Henry David Thoreau (1854) REBIRTH Treasure Island Robert Louis Stevenson (1883) DISCONTENT Death In Venice Thomas Mann (1912) DISEASE A Passage To India E.M. Forster (1924) UNREST Brave New World Aldous Huxley (1932) CONTROL The Heart Is A Lonely Hunter Carson McCullers (1940) TRAGEDY The Stranger Albert Camus (1943) OPPRESSION The Plague Albert Camus (1947) DEATH

RAIN

JEOPARDY Sense and Sensibility Jane Austen (1811) Ode On Melancholy John Keats (1819) MELANCHOLIA Fahrenheit 451 Ray Bradbury (1953) CATHARSIS The Grapes Of Wrath John Steinbeck (1939) HOPE Poisonwood Bible Barbara Kingsolver (1998) BAPTISM The Big Sleep Raymond Chandler (1939) FOREBODING

FOG

The Strange Case Of Dr Jekyll And Mr Hyde Robert Louis Stevenson (1886) FOREBODING Rebecca Daphne Du Maurier (1938) CONFUSION Bleak House Charles Dickens (1853) OPPRESSION The Woman In Black Susan Hill (1983) FOREBODING Hamlet William Shakespeare (1603-1607) STASIS The Fog James Herbert (1975) PSYCHOSIS The Fall Of The House Of Usher Edgar Allan Poe (1839) FOREBODING Party Going Henry Green (1939) STASIS

A WORLD OF **CRIME**

From London and Los Angeles to Ystad and Botswana, most of the world's popular serial literary detectives, whether police, private or amateur, are synonymous with a particular city. While Miss Marple, Hercule Poirot, Lord Peter Wimsey and Jack Reacher are wanderers, these detectives stay put, by and large.

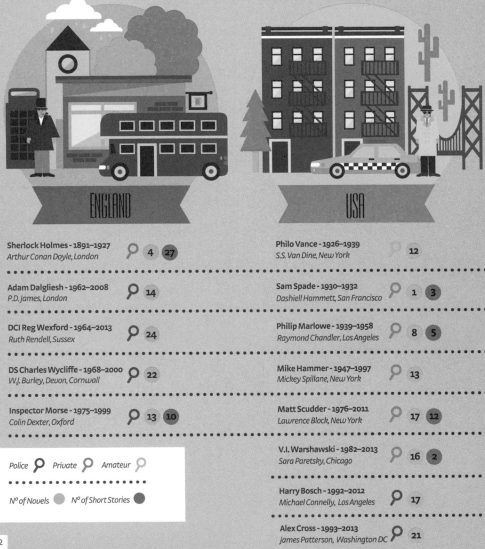

ENGLAND

USA

Sherlock Holmes - 1891–1927
Arthur Conan Doyle, London — 4 · 27

Philo Vance - 1926–1939
S.S. Van Dine, New York — 12

Adam Dalgliesh - 1962–2008
P.D. James, London — 14

Sam Spade - 1930–1932
Dashiell Hammett, San Francisco — 1 · 3

DCI Reg Wexford - 1964–2013
Ruth Rendell, Sussex — 24

Philip Marlowe - 1939–1958
Raymond Chandler, Los Angeles — 8 · 5

DS Charles Wycliffe - 1968–2000
W.J. Burley, Devon, Cornwall — 22

Mike Hammer - 1947–1997
Mickey Spillane, New York — 13

Inspector Morse - 1975–1999
Colin Dexter, Oxford — 13 · 10

Matt Scudder - 1976–2011
Lawrence Block, New York — 17 · 12

V.I. Warshawski - 1982–2013
Sara Paretsky, Chicago — 16 · 2

Police | Private | Amateur

Nº of Novels | Nº of Short Stories

Harry Bosch - 1992–2012
Michael Connelly, Los Angeles — 17

Alex Cross - 1993–2013
James Patterson, Washington DC — 21

EUROPE

C. Auguste Dupin - 1841–1844
Edgar Allan Poe, Paris - France 🔍 3

Jules Maigret - 1931–1972
Georges Simenon, Paris - France 🔍 75 28

Aurelio Zen - 1988–2007
Michael Dibdin, Rome - Italy 🔍 11

Com Salvo Montalbano - 1994–2014
Andrea Camilleri, Sicily - Italy 🔍 20 40

Martin Beck - 1965–1975
Maj Sjowall, Per Wahloo, Stockholm - Sweden 🔍 10

Kurt Wallander - 1997–2013
Henning Mankell, Ystad - Sweden 🔍 12 1

DI Henk Grijpstra & DS Rinus de Gier - 1975–1997
Janwillem van de Wetering, Amsterdam, Netherlands 🔍 14

Arkady Renko - 1981–2013
Martin Cruz Smith, Moscow - Russia 🔍 8

DI Rebus - 1987–2013
Ian Rankin, Edinburgh - Scotland 🔍 19 23

Harry Hole - 1997–2013
Jo Nesbø, Oslo - Norway 🔍 10

Erlendur Sveinsson - 1997–2012
Arnaldur Indriðason, Reykjavík - Iceland 🔍 14

Thóra Gudmundsdóttir - 2005–2012
Yrsa Sigurdardóttir, Reykjavík - Iceland 🔍 8

OTHER

Ci Chen Cao - 2000–2013
Qiu Xiaolong, Shanghai - China 🔍 8

Benny Griessel - 2004–2011
Deon Meyer, Cape Town - South Africa 🔍 3

Precious Ramotswe - 1988–2007
Alexander McCall Smith, Gaborone - Botswana 🔍 14

Shunsaku Morie - 1990–2013
Taku Ashibe, Osaka - Japan 🔍 16 50

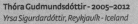

153

DICKENS' **LONDON**

*More than any other author, Charles Dickens mapped England's capital city
in his novels, and while many districts reappear in different novels, some
are specific to the stories of Oliver Twist, David Copperfield and Pip*

Where and how many times action
happened in particular postcode

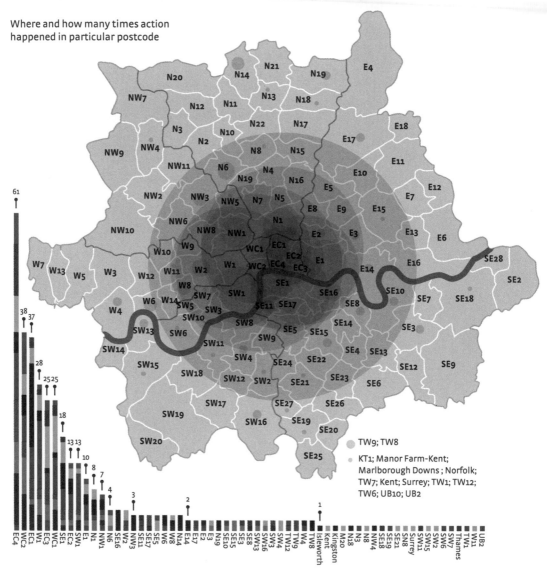

TW9; TW8

KT1; Manor Farm-Kent;
Marlborough Downs ; Norfolk;
TW7; Kent; Surrey; TW1; TW12;
TW6; UB10; UB2

In what area and how many times action from each book happened

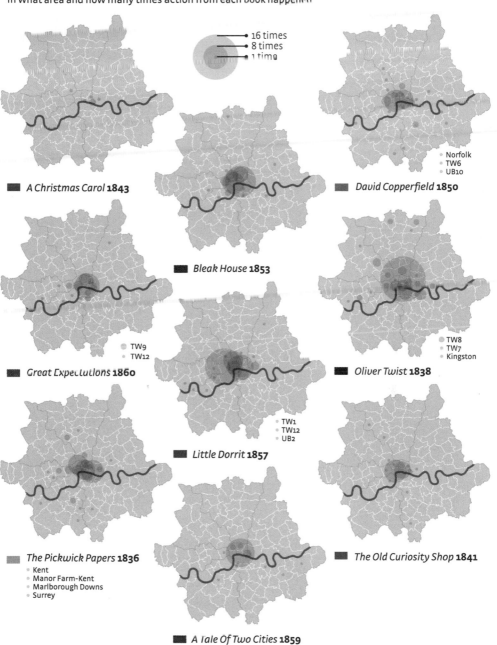

16 times
8 times
1 time

A Christmas Carol **1843**

David Copperfield **1850**
- Norfolk
- TW6
- UB10

Bleak House **1853**

Great Expectations **1860**
- TW9
- TW12

Oliver Twist **1838**
- TW8
- TW7
- Kingston

Little Dorrit **1857**
- TW1
- TW12
- UB2

The Pickwick Papers **1836**
- Kent
- Manor Farm-Kent
- Marlborough Downs
- Surrey

The Old Curiosity Shop **1841**

A Tale Of Two Cities **1859**

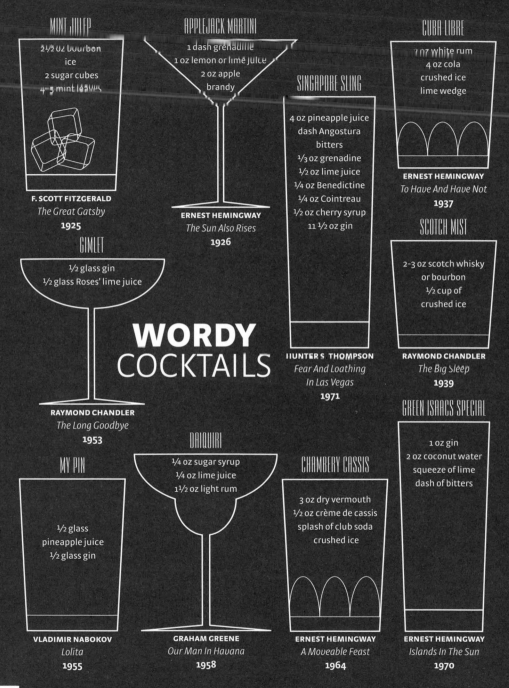

WORDY COCKTAILS

MINT JULEP
2 1/2 oz bourbon
ice
2 sugar cubes
4–5 mint leaves

F. SCOTT FITZGERALD
The Great Gatsby
1925

APPLEJACK MARTINI
1 dash grenadine
1 oz lemon or lime juice
2 oz apple
brandy

ERNEST HEMINGWAY
The Sun Also Rises
1926

CUBA LIBRE
2 oz white rum
4 oz cola
crushed ice
lime wedge

ERNEST HEMINGWAY
To Have And Have Not
1937

SINGAPORE SLING
4 oz pineapple juice
dash Angostura
bitters
1/3 oz grenadine
1/2 oz lime juice
1/4 oz Benedictine
1/4 oz Cointreau
1/2 oz cherry syrup
11 1/2 oz gin

HUNTER S. THOMPSON
*Fear And Loathing
In Las Vegas*
1971

SCOTCH MIST
2-3 oz scotch whisky
or bourbon
1/2 cup of
crushed ice

RAYMOND CHANDLER
The Big Sleep
1939

GIMLET
1/2 glass gin
1/2 glass Roses' lime juice

RAYMOND CHANDLER
The Long Goodbye
1953

MY PIN
1/2 glass
pineapple juice
1/2 glass gin

VLADIMIR NABOKOV
Lolita
1955

DAIQUIRI
1/4 oz sugar syrup
1/4 oz lime juice
1 1/2 oz light rum

GRAHAM GREENE
Our Man In Havana
1958

CHAMBERY CASSIS
3 oz dry vermouth
1/2 oz crème de cassis
splash of club soda
crushed ice

ERNEST HEMINGWAY
A Moveable Feast
1964

GREEN ISAACS SPECIAL
1 oz gin
2 oz coconut water
squeeze of lime
dash of bitters

ERNEST HEMINGWAY
Islands In The Sun
1970

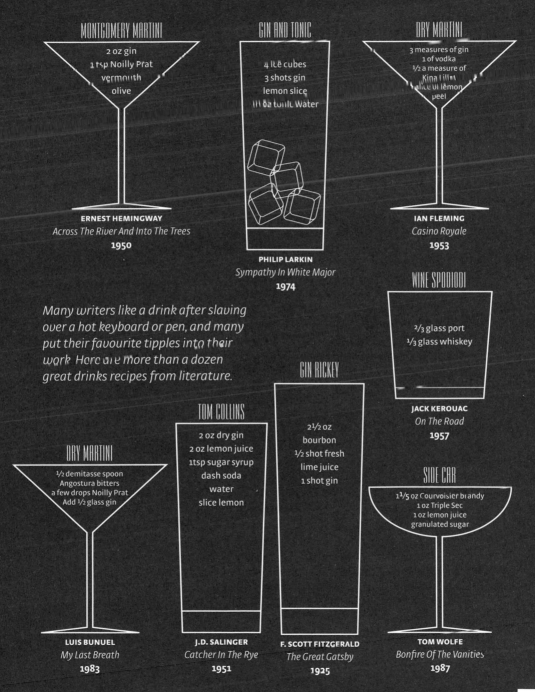

MONTGOMERY MARTINI

2 oz gin
1 tsp Noilly Prat
vermouth
olive

ERNEST HEMINGWAY
Across The River And Into The Trees
1950

GIN AND TONIC

4 ice cubes
3 shots gin
lemon slice
III oz tonic Water

PHILIP LARKIN
Sympathy In White Major
1974

DRY MARTINI

3 measures of gin
1 of vodka
½ a measure of
Kina Lillet
slice of lemon
peel

IAN FLEMING
Casino Royale
1953

WINE SPODIODI

⅔ glass port
⅓ glass whiskey

JACK KEROUAC
On The Road
1957

Many writers like a drink after slaving over a hot keyboard or pen, and many put their favourite tipples into their work. Here are more than a dozen great drinks recipes from literature.

DRY MARTINI

½ demitasse spoon
Angostura bitters
a few drops Noilly Prat
Add ½ glass gin

LUIS BUNUEL
My Last Breath
1983

TOM COLLINS

2 oz dry gin
2 oz lemon juice
1tsp sugar syrup
dash soda
water
slice lemon

J.D. SALINGER
Catcher In The Rye
1951

GIN RICKEY

2½ oz
bourbon
½ shot fresh
lime juice
1 shot gin

F. SCOTT FITZGERALD
The Great Gatsby
1925

SIDE CAR

1⅕ oz Courvoisier brandy
1 oz Triple Sec
1 oz lemon juice
granulated sugar

TOM WOLFE
Bonfire Of The Vanities
1987

FREE YOUR MIND

Since ancient times authors, poets and playwrights have been imprisoned by authorities who didn't like what they wrote. Of course putting a writer in a cell with nothing to distract them can result in great works of literature being incubated. Here are arguably the greatest prison-based works in history, and the reasons for their authors' imprisonment.

/ One day ✗ One month ⫽ One year

SEX

Thomas Wyatt (1503–1542)
Whoso List To Hunt (1557)
ADULTERY

Oscar Wilde (1854–1900)
De Profundis (1897)
GROSS INDECENCY

Eldridge Cleaver (1935–1990)
Soul On Ice (1968)
RAPE, ASSAULT WITH INTENT

Marquis de Sade (1740–1814)
The 120 Days Of Sodom (1785)
BLASPHEMY, SODOMY, RAPE

MONEY

John Cleland (1709–1789)
Memoirs Of A Woman Of Pleasure (1748)
DEBT

Henry David Thoreau (1817–1862)
Civil Disobedience (1849)
NON-PAYMENT OF TAXES

O. Henry (1862–1910)
Short Stories (1897–1901)
EMBEZZLEMENT

MURDER

Jack Abbott (1944–2002)
In The Belly Of The Beast (1981)
FORGERY, MURDER

WAR

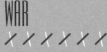

Arthur Koestler (1905–1983)
Scum Of The Earth (1941)
P.O.W.

Primo Levi (1919–1987)
If This Is A Man (1947)
P.O.W.

Miguel de Cervantes (1547–1616)
Don Quixote part I (1605)
P.O.W.

RELIGION

John Bunyan (1628–1688)
The Pilgrim's Progress (1675)
BREACHES OF THE RELIGION ACT 1592

Thomas Malory (1415–1471)
Le Morte d'Arthur (1451–1461)
ROBBERY, RAPE, TREASON

POLITICS

Aleksandr Solzhenitsyn (1918–2008)
One Day In The Life Of Ivan Denisovich (1962)
ANTI-SOVIET PROPAGANDA

Fyodor Dostoevsky (1821–1881)
The House Of The Dead (1861)
**DISSEMINATING REVOLUTIONARY
LITERATURE**

Nawal el-Saadawi (1931–)
Memories From The Women's Prison (1983)
POLITICAL SUBVERSION

Mahmoud Dowlatabadi (1940–)
Missing Soluch (1979)
POLITICAL SUBVERSION

Liu Xiaobo (1955–)
*The Monologues Of A Doomsday's
Survivor (1993)*
POLITICAL SUBVERSION

Richard Lovelace (1618–1657)
To Althea, From Prison (1642)
SEDITION

Daniel Defoe (1659–1731)
Hymn To The Pillory (1703)
SEDITIOUS LIBEL

Václav Havel (1936–2011)
Letters To Olga (1979–1982)
DISSIDENT

Boethius (AD480–525)
Consolation Of Philosophy (AD524)
TREASON

Ezra Pound (1885–1972)
The Prison Cantos (1948)
TREASON

Breyten Breytenbach (1939–)
*The True Confessions Of An
Albino Terrorist (1983)*
HIGH TREASON

Voltaire (1694–1778)
Oedipus (1717)
INSULTING THE CROWN

Niccolo Machiavelli (1469–1527)
The Prince (1513)
CONSPIRACY

Antonio Gramsci (1891–1937)
The Prison Notebooks (1928–1934)
CONSPIRACY

THEFT

Malcolm Braly (1925–1980)
On The Yard (1967)
THEFT, BURGLARY, ROBBERY

Jean Genet (1910–1986)
Our Lady Of The Flowers (1943)
THEFT

Chester Himes (1909–1980)
To What Red Hell (1931)
ARMED ROBBERY

François Villon (c.1431–c.1463)
The Testament Of 1461
BURGLARY

OTHER

Jack London (1876–1916)
The Road (1907)
VAGRANCY

Credits

Produced by Essential Works Ltd
essentialworks.co.uk

Essential Works

Art Director: Gemma Wilson
Commissioning Editor:
Mal Peachey
Editor: Julia Halford
Researchers: Naomi Barton,
George Edgeller, Phil Hunt,
Jane Mosely, Maria Ines Pinheiro,
Kimberley Simpson, Renske Start,
Jackie Strachan, Giulia Vallone,
Barney White.
Layout: Louise Leffler

Octopus Books

Editorial Director:
Trevor Davies

Production Controller:
Sarah-Jayne Johnson

Designers/Illustrators

Meegan Barnes (16–17)
Giulia De Amicis (34–35, 132–133)
Barbara Doherty (10–11, 14–15,
18–19, 28–29, 32–33, 38–39,
40–41, 58–59, 60, 66–67,
70–71, 82–83, 84–85, 100–101,
110–111, 130–131)
Jennifer Dossetti (21)
Maya Eilam (44–45)
Cristian Enache (12–13, 50–51,
52–53, 64–65, 68–69, 102–103,
104–105, 120–121, 128–129)
Dan Geoghegan (72–73, 74–75,
98–99)
Marco Giannini (62–63, 88–89,
112–113)
Wojciech Grabalowski (24–25,
80–81, 136–137)
Michael Gray (61, 108, 124–125)
Lorena Guerra (20, 22–23,
122–123, 138–139, 147)
Natasha Hellegouarch (142–143,
152–153)
Diana Coral Hernandez (56–57,
114–115)
Tomasz Kłosinski (46–47, 154–155,
158–159)
Stephen Lillie (26–27, 90–91,
106–107, 116)
Mish Maudsley (86–87)
milkwhale.com (54–55)
Aleksander Savic (140–141,
144–145)
Daniele Severo (36–37, 92–93)
Yael Shinkar (48–49, 126–127,
148–149)
Arnold Skawinski (42–43, 78–79)
Berny Tan (96–97)
Ryan Welch (30–31, 109)
Gemma Wilson (117, 118–119,
134–135, 146, 150–151, 156–157)
Anil Yanik (76–77, 94–95)

Answers to page 90–91

Author	Decade of key work	Nationality
Michel de Montaigne	1580–1590	French
Stendhal	1830–1840	French
Edgar Allan Poe	1840–1850	American
Gustave Flaubert	1850–1860	French
Leo Tolstoy	1865–1875	Russian
Mark Twain	1870–1880	American
August Strindberg	1880–1890	Swedish
Henrik Ibsen	1880–1890	Norwegian
Rudyard Kipling	1894–1894	English
Marcel Proust	1910–1920	French
Ernest Hemingway	1925–1935	American
Gunter Grass	1955–1965	German
VS Naipaul	1960–1970	Trinidadian
Robertson Davies	1970–1980	Canadian
Karl Ove Knausgaard	2000–1910	Norwegian

Answers to page 106–107

Author	Prime period	Nationality
Jane Austen	1800–1815	English
Mary Shelley	1818–1830	English
Elizabeth Barret Browning	1840–1850	American
George Sand	1830–1860	French
Colette	1900–1945	French
Virginia Woolf	1915–1940	English
Karen Blixen	1926–1956	Danish
Simone de Beauvoir	1940–1970	French
Doris Lessing	1950–1990	English
Maya Angelou	1970–1980	American
Toni Morrison	1980–2000	American
Herta Muller	1980–2000	German/Romanian
Donna Tartt	1992–2013	American
J.K. Rowling	1997–2007	English
E.L. James	2011–2013	English